BEING ALICE

(IN A WORLD LOST IN THE LOOKING GLASS)

MICHÈLE OLSON

Being Alice (In a world lost in the looking glass)

A Mackinac Island Story (Book Three)

Michèle Olson

Published by Lake Girl Publishing LLC, Green Bay, WI

www.LakeGirlPublishing.com

info@LakeGirlPublishing.com

Library of Congress Control Number: 2021903335

ISBN 978-1-7343628-7-9 (Paperback)

ISBN 978-1-7343628-8-6 (eBook)

ACKNOWLEDGMENTS

Book Cover Design: Karen Kalbacher

Arch Rock Painting: Michèle Olson

Interior Layout: Raymond A. Olson II

Editor: Emerald Barnes

Proofreader: Marlene Kane

Song, "Raincheck": Benjamin Olson

First Edition: 2021, printed in the U.S.A

A special thank you to my son Benjamin Olson, a singer song-writer out of Nashville, who allowed me to use his lyrics for the fictional character of J.D. in this novel. Hear "Raincheck" on iTunes here:

https://music.apple.com/us/album/rain-check-single/1578185525

and

You Tube here: https://bit.ly/3iIP3RG

Just a few of my favorites by Benjamin Olson:
"Sun Will Shine"
"Ordinary"
"There are Angels"

Dedication

To every teacher, pastor, priest, speaker, or person who took the time to tell me more about God, Jesus, The Holy Spirit, and the Bible — Thank you for speaking out. Your words made a difference.

To all the "Dan Fans", a hug and a wink. I know you appreciate the music of Dan Fogelberg as much as I do.

To all the musicians and singer songwriters who have made my life so much better because of your music. That includes James Taylor, Carly Simon, Carole King, Cat Stevens, Joni Mitchell, John Denver, Crosby, Stills, & Nash, Simon & Garfunkel, Fifth Dimension, America, Amy Grant, Bee Gees, Jackson Browne, The Beatles, and too many others to mention. Thank you for the music.

To my family, my friends, and all my encouragers — especially my faithful prayer warrior, Maxine.

To my husband Ray who works alongside me to keep the dream of Lake Girl Publishing, Fueling Faith with Fiction™. Thank you for your loyalty and love.

Don't Miss the Goodies in the Back of the Book!

This is the third book in my Mackinac Island Story series. The book stands on its own as a single offering; however, you will find it an even richer story if you read the first book in the series: *Being Ethel (In a world that loves Lucy)* where we meet Piper Penn for the first time. The next book in the series is *Being Dorothy (In a world longing for home)* where Piper Penn meets a mysterious couple on the porch of the Grand Hotel. But are they who they seem to be? It's a story with a James Bond flare.

Also, if you can and have enjoyed any of my books:

▪ Leave a review at all the big book sites. This makes an author's day and helps me be found by other readers in the mass world of books! Good reviews also counteract internet trolls who sometimes say unkind things without even reading the book.

▪ Give these books as gifts! Share the eBook and/or paperback versions with friends and family for birthdays and "just because." **Fuel Faith with Fiction™!**

▪ Join me on social media. All contacts are listed in this book.

Plus! Listen to the song mentioned in this novel. How cool is that?

And now, dive into this treasure. It's written with your reading enjoyment in mind — straight from my heart!

Blessings,
Michèle

I love to hear from readers!
info@lakegirlpublishing.com

THE FORGET-ME-NOT

LEGEND

A French knight was walking along a river with his lady. He bent
down to pick her a pretty little blue flower, but his heavy armor
caused him to lose his balance and he fell into the current.
Before sinking forever, he tossed the flower to his lady, shouting
"ne m'oubliez pas" (forget-me- not)! And that's the legend of
how the forget-me-not got its name.

CHAPTER ONE

SUMMER 1981

"You owe me."

I know he's right, but I can't agree to this. It's too much for me. Couldn't he be more sensitive just this once? Especially after all he's seen me go through?

"Did you hear me, Alice Merveille? I took you and your mother in when the state was about to split you up and take you away. You'd be heaven-knows-where if it wasn't for me. And then all those medical bills!"

"But Uncle Rabbit, since the accident — my face! I could still get the money somehow to pay you back. Isn't it bad enough my mom is gone? I'm already struggling …"

I can't believe I'm still calling my pseudo-uncle by the name I used for him when I was little, but he goes bat crazy if I call him anything else. I can't count all the names for him that come in my mind every day, and they are far from endearing. Now, I have to listen to him drone on. How convenient for him that anytime he wants to rant, he plants himself in my doorway. With a bedroom at the back of his music store, I am the captive audience for his babbling anytime he feels like it.

"It is what it is. I shouldn't have to remind you — I'm not your blood relative." His face turns even redder as he continues his rant. "Your dad was adopted, and we didn't even get along. When your mother called me, I must have had a weak moment or something. And, then, you were so little and called me Uncle Rabbit. Robert is such a boring name; I like Uncle Rabbit. I should have known better than to fall for your mom's sob story."

"But look how hard I've worked to make the music shop prosperous, especially before the accident. It was really going well …"

"Yes, it was on the uptick. But that darn recession hit and who could afford musical instruments anymore? Not a necessity in most people's minds. It might have been okay if your mother's medical bills hadn't kept coming from that blasted cancer. And then, the car accident, and all your medical bills," he says.

"She couldn't help getting sick, and the accident, well …"

"Yeah, yeah, yeah, I've heard it all before from you. Listen, another chance like this won't come along in a million years. It won't be so bad. You are only bound to work this gig for part of the summer. All the instruments they're renting can go to auction afterward for a handsome profit. People love it when a big-name artist or band has played an instrument. Collectors will bid big. Make a note to try to get some signatures on the guitars. With that and selling the store, I'll finally have enough money to close up this dang shop and retire. You're old enough to go on your way. Our time as relatives is over. I'm tired. This hasn't been no tea party for me, you know."

"I'm grateful. Really, I am. Oh, but my face! The world isn't the same for me anymore."

"So, it's mangled. It happened. I'm sorry it had to happen, but to be blunt, half of it still looks good. Just watch how you approach people. If you let them see your normal side first, maybe they won't be so reactive. Hey, why not wear a patch with a veil coming down from it? You could come off as exotic, like someone in a circus freak show."

I wish he knew what an idiot he sounds like. I'm the tired one. Tired of having to act eternally grateful every minute of every day. Tired of having nowhere to turn but to this crazy person.

"The label somehow got wind of your exceptional musical genius. Some guy who talked to a guy who saw what you can do. Plus, we're close enough to the island. You've been there tons of times. Have you ever even had the money to go inside the Grand and take a tour?" he asks.

"No. I've only seen it from the outside."

"See, that's already better. You can go inside and tour to your heart's content. Famous hotel. Famous rock guy. You should be thanking me, not giving me dirty looks."

"But Uncle Rabbit …"

"Not to mention, you've had J.D. Grayling's poster on the inside of your closet door forever. You'll finally get the chance to road manage his instruments. I'll never understand where it comes from, but we both know you can tune any instrument in your sleep. Maybe they'll even want you to play."

"Me? Play with them? Yeah, right. So, I had a few rock stars' posters in my bedroom, so does every other junior high girl at some point."

"Uh, you put up his poster on the back of your closet door when his first album came out in 1972, and you were twenty years old. Remember when the store vacuum went on the fritz, and I had to get the one from the house? It got it out of your closet, and I saw his poster. There he was, staring right at me. Rock stars. Good luck with those egos. I think you have a big crush on him. I've heard you playing his songs many a night. You must know his whole catalog, and every instrument on every album. You should be ecstatic that this has come along."

"I would have been before …"

"Life goes on, Alice. And right now, I want my debts paid off and *my* life to go on in Florida. I wanna be one of those guys who wears white shoes, sits around, and does nothing all day but complain about the government. Goodbye obligations, responsibilities, and dealing with people day after day. I'm not a fan of people."

"So, when I am done with the gig, then you'll be gone and the store, too? What am I supposed to do then? Working in this store is the only job I've had since I was seventeen – since the accident. Who wants to hire me looking like this?"

"You'll figure something out. It's time you grew up. You're almost thirty years old for Pete's sake. If that accident wouldn't have happened, you would have made such a name for yourself with your talent. Man, it's been almost twelve years already. Seems impossible. I would have kicked you out years ago. You and your mother have been nothing but a money drain. You're lucky I felt sorry for you."

"I appreciate all you did for me and my mom, Uncle Rabbit, but I'm scared."

"Of course, you're scared. Look at the positives. You'll be living at the Grand Hotel for part of the summer, and you're going to be working for your favorite rock star. Most people would be thrilled. Besides, afterward, you can get a job somewhere giving kids music lessons or something. I've never seen anyone who can play as many instruments as you can, or as well as you play. But I'm not going to sugarcoat it. No one is going to want that face on stage. Now sign the contract already. You have a week to get there and have all the instruments ready to go before he and his entourage arrive. They'll get used to how you look. I did. The regulars here at the store hardly even stare anymore. I don't deny you were dealt a bum hand, but you have to live the hand you were dealt or in your case, the face."

After all these years, I don't flinch as much as I did in the beginning when he says cruel things. I've longed for a way to get out from under his grip, but I've never had the courage to try. It's just been easier to stay here and keep to myself. And somehow, the finances always showed unending debt for me and my mom. She told me all the time that we owed our lives to this man, that without him, we would have been homeless.

"Looks aren't everything. Now sign and start packing. You'll look back on this someday and see I did the right thing."

"Then, if I do this, we're square? My mother and my debts are paid off?"

"I'm sure you still owe me, but I'll call it even. Sign right here. It's time for both of us to get on with our lives. I'm not getting any younger."

As I sign the contract, I wish this had come along when I was seventeen before all these years of pain and loneliness. Uncle Rabbit is right about one thing; I have been crazy about J.D. Grayling since he put out his first album. I can play every song he's ever written on any instrument. And now I get the chance to finally meet this gorgeous man, and instead of my heart's desires coming true, I have to witness an ironic retelling of *Beauty and the Beast*. Only this isn't a fairy tale, it's my life. Maybe I will make a patch or a veil. It would be even better if I could be like the other Alice and fall down a rabbit hole. Maybe I could enter a world where I don't look like this.

What do you hold for me Mackinac Island and Grand Hotel? Do you have shadows where I can hide and play music but not be seen? How can a dream coming true be a nightmare all at the same time?

CHAPTER TWO

Two suitcases. Two large, shabby, thrift store suitcases, but still, just two. I don't know what it says about me that I can fit my life in two rectangular boxes. Uncle Rabbit made it clear he was emptying the store quickly and moving on, so there would be no storage for me.

"Box it up, and I'll haul it to the church thrift shop, or it's going in the trash," he said.

Such finesse.

It helps that my room is a big closet attached to a little closet. To think that this run-down little hovel has been my home since I was seven, and we landed on his doorstep. At least here, we were able to stop chasing cockroaches and itching from bedbugs after staying in cheap Detroit motels. Mom said not to complain. Dad taking off in the middle of the night meant we had to take whatever help we could get.

"This is against my better judgment, but you can live in the back storage room of my store. If you're willing to work, you can live there for free." That's the greeting we got when we arrived at Uncle Rabbit's music store.

It was the first time I met him. That scrunchy, grouchy face hasn't changed since that initial encounter. All the time it took for my mom and me to hitchhike up into the Upper Peninsula of Michigan and land in Cheboygan made Detroit seem like a distant memory. Every chance she got; she plugged the virtues of living with her brother-in-law. I don't remember meeting the guy, but she made him sound like a great uncle. Looking back, I can see why she couldn't support me on her own. Employers don't appreciate slightly drunk people showing up occasionally for work.

Even if he was mostly a jerk to us, my mother never let me forget he was the reason we had a roof over our heads and food on our table. If she was being totally honest, she should have added — and wine in her coffee cup. I think until the day she passed, she thought she pulled off hiding her alcohol. At least she kept it together enough to keep Uncle Rabbit off our case until she was diagnosed with cancer. Once the treatments started, she was a bigger mess. He had enough scruples to see her through to the end, but not without constant complaining.

Hmm. I wonder how long he's been scheming to sell the store and get rid of me. Sending me on my way, getting a wad of cash, and being done with the store are the perfect storm of indulging his "me, me, me" world where he exists as king.

Maybe it's for the best. Knowing me, I would never leave. I've daydreamed about it a million times, but then I catch a glimpse of myself in the mirror and the bubble bursts.

"You're lucky to be alive," the ER doctor said.

That is not my definition of lucky, Marcus Welby. Cheated? Yes, that's closer. Cheated out of a future that matters. But I had some good moments in this tiny town and this goofy music store. With every restringing of a guitar, violin, or cello, I felt, well, happy—like I was worth something. I couldn't help but smile at the look on the face of a school kid getting an instrument they've dreamed about. No one can ever take away from me the joy of playing. I love being lost in the quarter notes and an arpeggio. I'm just me, not me with a weirdo's face. I hate how much it meant to me to hear Uncle Rabbit brag to customers how he's never seen anyone who can do what I do on any instrument.

He's a jerk, but he does know music. I've lost count of all the stories about his life in the music world of the 60s and 70s. According to him, all the big names came to him for advice at one time or another. Right. Too bad no one has told him his faded tattoos, scraggly ponytail, and hippie vibe aren't doing him any favors.

Oh, yes! Perfect timing, a J.D. Grayling song on the radio! I've gotta turn this up and soak it in. Yes! His big hit, and thank you very much, I can sing every word right along with him. Ahh … I love the title too – *"Raincheck."*

Can I get a rain?
Can I get a raincheck on you?
If it's all the same
Can I get a raincheck on you?
We used to be wise
Analyze what we do
What's wrong with the fool?
Play it cool with the truth
All we want is just to feel alive
Waiting for this moment to arrive
All we have is …. Time, time, time
Time, time, time
Can I get a rain?
Can I get a raincheck on you?
I've got myself to blame.
Can I get raincheck on you?
I'm locked in a dream; you'll be locked in one soon
The tides moving in and the rains comin' too
All we want is just to feel alive
Waiting for this moment to arrive
All we have is time, time, time
Time, time, time, time
Time, time, time

Time, time, time, time
All we want is just to feel alive
Waiting for this moment to arrive
All we have is time, time, time
Time, time, time
Time, time, time
Time, time, time

I love singing with him on the radio! It's such a crowd-pleaser, and I'm going to meet him! I'll be tuning the instruments he'll be playing. I'm getting goosebumps. I get to take care of the on-stage details for his rockin' band, The Mad Hatters. Ladies and Gentlemen! The Grand Hotel is proud to present for your listening pleasure, J.D. Grayling, and The Mad Hatters! Please pay no attention to the unsightly mess who has all these instruments in tune —she lost half her face, and she's hideous. But, hey, she can tune a mean guitar!

Oh, great. Uncle Rabbit is knocking on my door, probably to tell me to turn down my radio.

"Come in. It's open."

"Are you going deaf? I swear, I never knew someone who has to blare a radio louder than you," he says.

"Sorry, well, you won't have to deal with me much longer. I'll be gone soon," I say.

"Here," he says, handing me a book.

"What's this?" I ask.

"I took some boxes over to the church thrift drop-off, and the lady said they were giving out modern Bibles — whatever that is."

"You can have it. You brought the boxes over."

"No thanks. I'm too old for religion. You take it."

"Okay. I'll put it in my suitcase. I could use some God help."

"You'll be fine. Quit griping. Just stay in the shadows, do your music thing, and don't forget to get the instruments signed before you have them sent to the auction house at the end of the gig. And, for Pete's sake, don't make a fool of yourself drooling over poster guy when you meet him. I want the full payment amount at the end, and I can't afford for you to screw any of this up. And another thing you can thank me for, is that you can stay at the Grand Hotel. It's in the contract. They gave me grief because only the star and the manager usually stay there. The rest of his entourage stay at dormitory-style housing a few blocks away, but I pushed back."

"I'm staying at the Grand? Really? I never thought that would happen to me. Thank you for arranging that," I say.

"My going away gift to you. Emphasis, going away."

Even when he's trying to do something halfway decent, he wrecks it.

"Yeah, well, it might not be their biggest room, but at least you can stay on the grounds and not subject the people in town to that face of yours walking around," he says.

So, there's the motivation. He's afraid I'll scare people. I hope this is the last time I ever see that sick smirk that always puts a knot in my stomach. Okay, God, does it say anywhere in my new Bible why I ended up in the care of this crackpot? Sending me on my way is the best thing he has ever done for me. And I don't think I can keep my promise. It will take every ounce of my willpower not to drool when I meet Mr. J.D. Grayling.

CHAPTER THREE

It's like stepping into a hot shower on a cold winter's day. You know you're going to love it and not want to get out, but you have to shut off the water at some point. And then the chills come back, and you wish it never had to end. That's what I think my time on the island is going to be like. I can't wait to get in and meet everyone, but once they see me, and the gig's over —all I'll be left with is that chilly, sad feeling and nowhere to belong. But here I am, taking the ferry to Mackinac. I'm scared to death.

I had no idea when the ferry dumped us off on the island for our yearly school trip for "Mackinac Day" as they called it that someday I would be spending weeks on the island, let alone at the Grand. If younger me touring Fort Mackinac for free could see into the future and realize I would be staying at that magnificent hotel — well, I'm still flabbergasted! The Fort was a thrill at the time. I still remember the tour guide's spiel — *Fort Mackinac is the former British and American military outpost garrisoned from the late eighteenth century to the late nineteenth century.* Then they would tell us stories of the real people who lived there. Man, those guides sure had to memorize a lot. We got to see the firing of the cannon, some guns, and how the soldiers lived day-to-day life in

Fort Mackinac. Those trips were the first time I thought I might work on the island in the summers as a tour guide or maybe be the fife player in the reenactment if they would ever let a girl take the part.

With the three dollars my mom gave me to spend on the trip, I made sure to pick out something that had the words "Mackinac Island" somewhere on my trinket. I hoped when I used my treasure at home, I would recapture those island feelings. Silly, but it did make me feel better every time I used my souvenir big pencil or drank out of the small cup.

It was Peggy, always bold Peggy, who talked me into sneaking away from our class and walking up the street to get a closer look at the Grand Hotel porch. It looked enormous, like something in a fairy tale or a Hollywood movie. For weeks after we got back that year, I dreamed of staying there and meeting a handsome prince who would whisk me away to his foreign castle until we returned for our yearly stay at the Grand. Peggy and I talked about it for the last few weeks of school. Once she moved away, I never had the courage to sneak away from the group. What a goofy kid I was. *Wake up, Alice — pay attention to the scenery.* There it is. The Grand in the distance. It's the perfect name for this magnificent white wonder of architecture.

"Oh, did you have to have eye surgery at your age? I wore a patch once too when I got a scratch on my retina. That was painful. I didn't have a veil with my patch though, that's kind of interesting."

Oh great. Why is there always a nosy lady in every group of people I ever meet? This one doesn't believe in combing your hair or matching clothes.

"Uh, no, I had an accident, and this protects my face," I say.

"Oh, a patch and a veil. Very piratey of you, and you are on a boat…arrgggghhhh. Am I right?" she persists getting way too close to my face and doing the worst imitation of a pirate I've ever heard.

"I, uh, don't, um …," I say. Please go away lady. I wish I could think of what to say to not cause a scene.

"Hey, I've been looking for you. I saved you a seat over here. Excuse us, please. We have a lot of catching up to do." Another lady is taking my arm, but I think she has confused me for someone else. Tugging my sleeve to keep me heading toward the back of the boat, I'm not sure what's happening. I don't think I know her.

"Hi, I'm Piper, and I hope you didn't mind me whisking you away from that lady. You looked as if you were feeling uncomfortable, and I don't blame you. So pushy!" Piper whispers.

"Oh, thank you. I was slow to catch on there, and yes, I didn't know what to do. I'm new to crowds. And I'm nervous to be heading to the island."

"Is it your first time?" she asks.

"No, well not really. I've lived in Cheboygan, you know, like just over twenty miles from here. We used to come the island for school every year, but we mostly went to the fort and the historic stuff. It's been a while since I've been here as an adult."

"Cool, then I bet you're excited. My heart skips a beat every time I leave, and the boat gets near. I don't leave very often, but sometimes I have to go to the mainland for business. Are you staying for a few days? I hope I'm not being too nosy."

"It's fine. Actually, I'm staying a few weeks. I have a behind-the-scenes part as the music tech for one of the summer concerts coming to the Grand."

"The J.D. Grayling concerts? Super cool! I love his music. I know a little about the concert coming, because my husband is the groundskeeper at the Grand. His name is Cam if you happen to run into him. He has the reddest red hair you've ever seen, so you can't miss him," she says.

"So, word is out about the concert? It should be great," I say.

"Yes, they think it will bring in a lot of new people to the island to see his music along with everything already here. I have a shop in town, so I keep up with most things happening on the island. You'll have to stop in," Piper says.

"I'm looking forward to seeing the shops in my free time. What's the name of your place?"

"The Creative Lilac. It's a place for creativity of all kinds, including art in different mediums—including my favorite, watercolor."

"You're an artist! I'd love to see your work. I love artwork," I say.

"Then you are perfect person to come for a visit. There's no limit really to what we offer. The store exists for all things people like to do such as crafts, knitting, crochet, and even a meeting place for some women's groups to hang out and encourage each other."

"It sounds like a place dreams are made of. I've worked in my uncle's music shop for years, but it was mostly stringing and retuning instruments for band kids and some town regulars," I say.

"So, you get all the wonderful things that can happen in a small shop. Every day is an adventure. We have so much fun. I'm sorry, I didn't even get your name!" she says.

"I'm Alice, Alice Merveille. Sorry, I must seem awkward to you. I'm not used to being out in public much, with my face as it is."

"Oh, please. You are beautiful, and I love how creatively you are wearing the patch and veil. Did you make that yourself?"

"Yes, out of necessity. I was in a terrible accident, and I'm not like other people."

"You need to meet my friend Sister Mary-Margaret. She's the one that showed me the real me, which has nothing to do with what you look like."

"Sister? A nun? Um, I don't go to church. I didn't mean to make my problem your problem," I say.

"And I'm not Catholic, but that has nothing to do with what I'm talking about. Listen to me babble on! Since you're going to be on the island for a few weeks, and I'm there too, you've now got your first island friend, if you'll have me?"

"Well, yes. That would be nice. I don't know anyone on the island. I haven't met the band yet. They'll be there shortly after me, I guess."

"Believe me, I know what you're feeling as you get closer to your first step on the island. I was in your shoes, feeling a lot of the same things you are just a few years ago. Now, here I am, married, owning a business, and an islander. And the best part is, I just found a new friend today. The day doesn't get better than that."

"Piper, right?"

"Yes, Piper Penn, which is the name I use in my business. My married name is Nelson. And that red head I mentioned is my husband Cam Nelson. See, you already know two people! And Sister Mary-Margaret is coming for a visit any day now. You'll have to meet her—you will love her. She's hilarious, fun, sincere, and stop me, because I am rattling on and not letting you get a word in edgewise!"

I can't believe it's me laughing out loud. Her face is lit up, and her arms are waving around with every new name she puts out. She's one of the most enthusiastic people I've ever met. My patch and veil don't seem to affect her. Maybe Uncle Rabbit was wrong. I won't scare people.

"Mom, look at the goofy lady! Look at her eye patch hanging down."

Oh joy, now I have a little critic to contend with.

"Mom, look at her. She's dressed up for Halloween and it's not Halloween!"

Mouthing the word "sorry," to me, I'm thankful his mother catches up with him and pulls him back toward the front of the boat.

Squeezing my hand, Piper whispers to me, "Alice, listen to me. Kids yell out crazy stuff —I see it in my shop all the time. Ignore that. You are about to have a wonderful summer, and we are going to have a fun time getting to know each other. Don't lose your excitement about how close we are to your first step on the island as an adult. Joy lies ahead. Don't let anything steal that from you."

I've never had someone say something so encouraging to me in my whole life. I hope Piper is right, but from what I've seen, there are a lot ruder little boys and Uncle Rabbits in the world than nice people. I don't know if I have the strength to fight them all.

CHAPTER FOUR

Unclench your fist, Alice. It's not going to fall out of your pocket. I'm treating this business card from Piper with her contact information like it's a rare four-leaf clover. Ahh, there's the Grand carriage. So beautiful! That's what Uncle Rabbit said to do when I got here. Find the carriage and get a ride to the hotel. If he hadn't told me my luggage would already be brought up there for me, I know I'd be standing here in even more of a panic. I don't know how all of this works. Dry mouth, sweaty palms — oh, I'm doing fine. Almost thirty, and never really took a suitcase anywhere. Yeesh, I am something else. Maybe I'll come off to people here as backward and awkward. Well, I should — I am! If it's not about music or books, I'm clueless. I feel it in my bones. This could all be a mistake. They all look like they've been around and know what to do. Who am I kidding? Once anyone sees the patch, they don't give the rest of me a second thought. Problem solved. Man, my nerves are through the roof! *Take a deep breath, Alice!*

It was nice of Piper to offer her help to get me get to the Grand, but that's embarrassing. I told her I knew what I was doing. Fat chance! There she goes, disappearing into the crowd who can't wait to begin their time on the island. Too late. I'm on my own. *Get with it, Alice! Move forward, one foot in front of the other.* This brisk wind off the water should make me feel cool, but instead—sweating palms like it's a sweltering summer day. Overwhelming, yes, that's the word to describe this moment. *Alice! Get your mind off yourself for five minutes and look around. You are on Mackinac Island, and you need to take in this place.*

If only the rational part of my brain would show up to yell at me more often. I need it. "Poor Me" brain tends to rule the day, and I fall back into my non-stop pity party. I'm sick of it. Uncle Rabbit has been no help, that's for sure. It's like I'm a bird let out of a cage for the first time who is not sure what to do. Oh, the *clip clop* of the horses and the sounds of the bikes here near the dock! It's like walking into another world — a world of fresh air and breezes flowing off The Straits. Maybe it will help to imagine the days and people long gone who have left a trail of remembrance. This place is oozing with history. And, yes, the many lilac trees will be bursting into bloom soon. To think, I'll be here for every glorious, fragrant moment. Yes, think of the lilacs. I'm remembering now — that one school trip when the island was in full bloom. Oh lilacs! You have filled many of my dreams with your purple glory and sweet smell. *Okay, Alice. Do what's next here.*

"Sir, I believe I should be taking this carriage to the Grand," I say to the gentlemen in the top hat by the carriage.

"Welcome, milady, it is my pleasure to welcome you to the island. If you would like to wait inside, I'll be here a few more minutes to see if there are any other guests to gather from this boat."

"Thank you, sir." Milady! And no strange stares at my face. He's a pro. I'll take it.

Stepping up into the carriage, I can't wait to see the inside. Okay, I get it. Seats along the outer edges where there are windows. Every time I caught a glimpse of a carriage going by when I was a kid, all I could think about was how lucky those people were. Now, it's me seeing the looks of tourists walking by, wishing they were sitting in this carriage clearly marked "Grand Hotel." It's my turn to feel like a princess! Never in my life did I imagine I would get this chance. Here's a pinch. Yes! This is really happening to me. *Think good thoughts, Alice.* Here comes another passenger. A gentleman, and he's moving to the opposite corner. I wonder if I should say something or not. I don't know the etiquette.

"Hello. Beautiful day," he says, tipping his fedora.

Good, he spoke.

"Hello, yes, it is a beautiful day," I say with a nod. He's rather distinguished, maybe late forties, pushing fifty, I'm not sure. With a bit of salt and pepper in his dark hair, I'm leaning toward picking forty-nine. He has, well, an air about him, like a person who should be going to the Grand. I do see the squint for a moment — he's probably perusing my patch with a veil. Maybe the veil is too much. I don't know. I wish I had someone to ask. I should have asked Piper. I think he's uncomfortable. At least that's what it feels like with the way he looked away quickly.

"First trip to the Grand?" I ask.

"Yes, business really. Quite a quaint place from what I've seen so far. Very lovely."

If this guy ever showed up in Cheboygan, he would have stood out. He's not from around here, that's for sure. But then I imagine most of the people going to the Grand aren't from the area. And, here we go, we are on the move. Ugh, I hope the guy didn't notice how much I jumped when the carriage lurched forward. I didn't realize we were leaving.

"Whoa, everything okay there?" he asks.

"Yes, thank you. I didn't know we were taking off." He noticed.

"Are you making some kind of statement with the face get up?" he asks.

Oh, change of tone. The way he said that, like he's mocking me.

"Face get up? Um, no …" I say softly.

"Takes all kinds, I guess," he says adjusting his fedora. "Yes, takes all kinds."

Wow, this guy has some nerve. That was rude! I should just shut up. Darn it, no! That was really mean. *Stand up for yourself for once, Alice!*

"Excuse me, but I'm not playing dress-up if that's what you're implying. I was in an accident, and my face doesn't look anything like the other side, so I hide it," I say.

"Well, it's your business. Too bad really. The other half of your face is somewhat acceptable."

Acceptable? Who is this guy? I have taken this kind of talk for years from Uncle Rabbit, but not you mister, not you. I'm tired of taking crap from guys like you.

"And I don't appreciate your tone and comments. Is it really your place to speak out about anything I'm wearing?"

Wow. I'm amazing myself. Island air is giving me courage or something. Who am I all of a sudden?

"Listen, it was just an observation. I've travelled extensively with important people, so I was passing some helpful information your way. If you want to fit in, it's best not to make a spectacle of yourself. That's all. You don't need to get your undies in a bundle. Lighten up," he says.

I had this guy all wrong. He doesn't belong at the Grand. A snarky creep, really. *Think, Alice!* Think up a zinger that will put this arrogant man in his place. Too late, here comes another couple boarding from the next ferry stop. Good. I'll let the conversation end with a dirty look and be done with this very miserable person. I had such a surge of chutzpah as my mom used to say, but as quickly as it came, it's fading. This couple now a part of our little entourage are talking enough for all of us. Besides, the Grand is a big place, I probably won't see him again. Works for me. Jerk!

"Matt! Isn't it amazing? We're in the Grand Hotel carriage. Let the fairy tale begin!" The lady with lighthouse earrings and the big red hat is waving her arms, pointing, and squealing at everything she sees. She's a welcome diversion from the tension in the air.

"Settle down, Maggie. It is nice, but don't scare these other guests in here. Sorry, folks, the Mrs. is subject to bursts of enthusiasm, as they say." Turning to the rude man with the fedora he leans in toward him when he talks. Oh, fussy fedora man isn't like that.

"We are both extremely excited to be on the island and even more excited to be staying at the Grand to see a J.D. Grayling concert! Have you heard he's going to be performing?" he asks.

"Yes, that is exciting. Glad to hear you're excited about the concert. It's always nice to meet fans of J.D.," the rude man says. He's suddenly turned the cordial back on for these fine folks.

"Oh, you're a fellow fan too?" Maggie asks the man.

"I guess you could say that. I'm his manager, Montague Cheshire."

Wait, what? This guy I just insulted is J.D.'s manager, the person I'm supposed to check in with when I get to the Grand— my new boss? Uh-oh.

CHAPTER FIVE

Of course, Matt and Maggie are exiting the carriage first. They are the closest to the door. I can't plow them over and run for it. Too bad! Do I pull the band-aid off and address this right now, or give it some time after checking in, hoping he is less irritated? My new life is getting off to a bumpy start. Par for my course.

"Um, Mr. Cheshire?"

"Oh, I'm worth speaking to, Miss High-and-Mighty? Don't tell me, you're a J.D. Grayling fan and now you're wondering if I can get you seats up front or a back-stage pass. Fat chance!"

"First, I'm sorry for my tone. I have dealt with a lot with my face, and I can be overly sensitive when I'm criticized."

"So touchy. I wasn't criticizing you, merely making an observation. It's a big world out there, maybe you should toughen up a bit. Since the probability of us seeing each other again is highly unlikely, I don't see the need to continue this conversation," he says as he turns to leave the carriage. Another sneer with raised condescending eyebrows.

"Well, the thing is—"

"Seriously, I have things to do. Good day."

"But, Mr. Cheshire, I'm ..."

And he's gone. Okay. Decision made for me. I'll tell him when he has cooled down a little. So, I get the nerve to speak some truth, and I stick my foot right in my mouth. But I'm not in the wrong here. This guy wrecked my magical ride to the Grand and now possibly my future. I have a right to be fuming!

Stepping out of the carriage, it's a relief he's not here anymore. I should check in, but I'm so shaky. *Settle down Alice, deep breaths. Calm down.* Maybe taking a moment to sit on the porch in one of these beautiful white wicker rocking chairs and regrouping is a good plan. It seems pretty quiet right now, so I shouldn't draw much attention. Yes, it seems like either way I look there's barely another person on the porch. Ah, the glorious water. The fresh air of the Straits. I knew the serenity of the Cheboygan River and Lake Huron all these years, but I don't think I've appreciated all that these bodies of water offer to soothe the soul. I want to do that this summer. I want to appreciate the water, the sky, the Mackinac Bridge, and yes, this island. Even with the Mr. Cheshire's in my life, I want to be in the moment.

Today I met Piper Penn. That's a good thing. I can use a friend, and her shop sounds like a wonderful place to hang out if I need a break from my new band life. Wait, could Montague fire me because of what happened, even before I even meet J.D.? Why does J.D. have such a guy working for him? He probably never shows that side of him to his boss, he saves it for the "little people," the nobodies. *Water, Alice. Sky, Alice. Fresh air, Alice. Deep breaths, Alice.* Oh my gosh, I didn't get it until now! His last name is Cheshire, like the Cheshire Cat in *Alice in Wonderland.* Freaky! Wouldn't it be nice if he would disappear out of this picture like the cat did in the story? A girl can hope. Alright, time to be a grownup. Get it together. I should go check in, get settled in my room, and then face the music. Boy, I'm full of double-entendres today. Face the music. I think check-in is on the bottom level under the porch, where the carriage let me off. Good thing the crowds are lighter this early in the season. I remember hearing that from coming over with my school group —one reason they let school groups visit. Makes sense. There's the check-in desk.

"Yes, reservation for Alice Merveille, please. I'm with the J.D. Grayling group, and I believe a room is set aside for me."

"Yes, Miss, let me check."

She's doing the double glance at my patch and veil. I think the veil has to go. The bottom half of the face more clearly explains the patch. I'll still get looks, but maybe they will be a little shorter. Or it will be the "glance and retreat" as I call it —a glance and then a fast look away.

"There you are. You have a room with a double bed on the second floor. I'm sorry, but outside rooms with windows and balconies are kept open for … well … paying guests."

"Oh, no problem. I'm thankful to have a room. Whatever you have set aside for me will be fine, I'm sure."

"Thank you for being understanding. I just checked in a gentleman a little while ago from your group who was less than thrilled with what was set aside. I wasn't sure what you were promised. We have a suite for J.D., but I guess that should be understandable, I mean, his being famous. We don't usually even have entourage members onsite so; these two rooms go beyond what we normally accommodate. This is probably more than you need to know," she added nervously. "I'm a little ruffled after that last encounter."

"Actually, I'm new to this group and haven't met the people yet ; however, I think I know who you are referring to. I didn't have the best interaction with him on the ride in. Probably more than you need to know."

With a big smile, our eyes meet in a mutual understanding of what we deal with way too often from other people.

"Well, thank you for being gracious. We want everyone staying here at the Grand to have a wonderful time. All of our rooms are beautiful and highly enjoyable. We make sure of that. There you are. Your bags will be outside your room when you get there. Here's your key, and I hope you enjoy the rest of your day and your stay here at the Grand. This little booklet is also your pass into the meals, which are part of your package. The food is amazing, so enjoy!"

"Thank you so much. You've made the day better already," I say, enjoying giving someone who obviously has to deal with a lot from people a big smile and appreciating her smile in return.

See? There are nice people in the world. You just have to look for them and ignore the meanies. New rule. Find the nice ones, skip the mean ones. Concentrate on the good. First Piper, and then the nice check-in lady. That beats out a grumpy artist manager any day. Besides, maybe he's having a bad day, and I hit him at the wrong moment.

Look around, Alice! The décor, wow! The carpeting here is amazing. Large flowers, large patterns, large statements when it comes to decorating. It all comes together. Now, up the elevator, down the hall a bit, and here. This is my new home. Key works great and oh my! She wasn't kidding! This is gorgeous and bigger than the room I've lived in for most of my life. A canopy bed with a floral top and curtains hanging down on each corner in soft pinks and pastel blues. Breathtaking! And the walls and curtains. Cotton candy pink that looks like delicate swirls of watercolor paint dancing on the walls. I've never seen a wallpaper like this, even in a magazine! The curtains flow like pink waves on the tops of the long windows facing out to the back of the building. Complain? I'm in heaven! I'll put up with a lot from the likes of the Mr. Cheshires in the world to get to stay in this room. Okay, I'll get my couple of dresses hung up, so the wrinkles fall out. Dressing up for dinner is out of my norm, but I know from eavesdropping on the tourists when I was a kid that it's required for dinner. Yeesh! These dresses may stick out more than my face, but I have what I have. Hopefully, the small weekly stipend promised in the contract will let me get a few things here on the island. It's not like I'm someone to display beauty anyway. I just don't want people to lose their appetites.

One black plain dress, one blue dress, and this most likely outdated flower print skirt will have to do.

Oh, look at the bathroom! The pink swirling is continuing in a zig zag pattern. This *is* a room fit for a princess. The Grand lives up to its reputation. There. Toiletries put away, things put in drawers, and I'm settled. Oh, fun— a little bottle of geranium shampoo, conditioner, and soap. Their signature flower is everywhere, right down to the soap.

Okay. Unpacking done. I'll have to see what I'm supposed to wear at concerts. I imagine if it's an evening concert, the crowd will be dressed for dinner, so dressed up. Any afternoon concerts are probably more casual. I have a lot to learn. The instruments must have arrived, and that should be my next step. I'll get directions to the concert hall and see where I'll be doing most of my work with everything. Hopefully, the hard work I put into packaging everything extra carefully will survive the horse drawn carriage ride here. Fingers crossed that every guitar and the drum set will be intact. Really? A knock at my door already. Who even knows I'm here? Oh, no! That voice on the other side of the door!

"Miss Merveille? I know we haven't met, but I'm J.D. Grayling's manager, and since we are both here early, I can give you directions for the concert hall."

Oh, how sickly sweet his voice is coming through the door when he doesn't know who I am. I wish I had a camera to capture the expression on his face when I open the door and he puts my name to my face.

"Miss Merveille. They told me you've checked in, so I thought I would introduce myself."

"Coming!" I say.

Oh, boy. Now, it's really time to face the music.

CHAPTER SIX

I f looks could kill, I might be dead. He had a fake happy
expression on his face for one second when I swung the door
open and now, it's gone.

"Oh, it's you!" he says.

"Yes, it's me. I tried to tell you as you were leaving the
carriage, but you went so quickly I didn't get a chance to tell you
my name. I'm Alice Merveille. I'm the guitar and instrument
tech that comes along with instruments."

"I was told you had excellent skills, but no one said anything
about your, well, condition," he says with what I've seen all too
often since I met him—a sneer.

"I'm sure you don't mean to be cruel, but what I have is not
a condition. As I told you in the carriage, I was in an accident,
and my face ended up looking like this. It has nothing to do with
my intellect, my mind, or my musical ability, which I assure you
is quite adequate," I say as firmly as I can.

"Yes, but we were hoping that if your musical prowess was
as astute as we had heard, you could fill in for some of the band,
if need be. You know … if someone is under the weather or gets
called away or such."

"Well, that will not be a problem. I can stay in the back and make sure the spotlight doesn't go anywhere near me, so I don't frighten any of the concert goers," I say.

I'm actually mortified to hear they think I would be on the stage playing an instrument. It's not a matter of knowing the music. But who would want to see me on stage? That scenario exists only in my made-up fantasies.

"We'll see. It may never even happen. It's simply good to have a backup, because as we all know – the show must always go on. You'll find the music room just off the stage in the main concert hall on the main floor, right past the small green room. I'm sure you can find it. I've not been there yet myself, but there's a map in the desk drawer that shows it clearly."

"You don't want to go down with me and look over everything?" I ask, knowing full well, he wants to get away from me as fast as he can.

"I can't right now. I have a place to be," he says looking at his watch.

Right. Two seconds ago, you wanted to go together, and now you are too busy. No one is here so far but us, but you have somewhere to be.

"Well, I hope we can put the carriage ride behind us, and I hope you can get past what you see as such a huge detriment — my face."

"Don't put words in my mouth. I'm sure you're, well, adequate. It's such a get-up with the veil. I mean a patch is quite enough. The veil is too much."

Darn. Now even though I was going to lose the veil, he will think it is because he said to.

"Yes, I was thinking perhaps it wasn't working and was planning on removing it and going with just the patch," I say. There, it isn't because you said so.

"That may be best. Whatever. The point is, you're here to make the instruments perfect. I don't really have anything to do with you besides that unless you have in mind to be a pest to J.D. Then, I will have something to say to you."

"Sir, I am a professional. I will be assisting Mr. Grayling as he needs for musical instruments, and that is all."

"That is good to hear. I don't imagine you will be sitting with the band at dinner. Well, what I'm saying is, make other plans. You should be able to find some other young lady staying here to eat with. You don't need to be at our table. We are used to travelling and being together, and I don't want you to feel as though you are part of what we do or what we have built. I know I'm being very blunt, but I find that is best."

"Oh, you are extremely clear that I am not welcome to be part of the group. I'll keep to myself and not trouble you," I say.

"Good to know we see eye-to-eye." There's another cold stare, and it's clear to me he knows exactly what he just said. It was intentional.

"I'm sure it's a good-old-boys club, and I wouldn't want to be the sole female messing up your tight knit group," I say getting ready to close the door.

"Oh, we aren't all men. J.D. is meeting his soon-to-be fiancé here—the niece of the hotel's owner — Vivian. She will be joining us soon. Such a lovely lady, a real head turner. She will be part of our group. A true beauty. We're already seven with the band, enough for one table at dinner, so just making sure you have a head's up."

"Aren't tables usually set for eight?" He's a jerk, but I might as well bait him a bit. He deserves it.

"Yes, but there will be various notable town guests or a fan or two who will probably join us. Not your concern. I'm sure you wouldn't feel comfortable with our group anyway. We have such a history. Again. Just making sure we understand each other. Afterall, I am J.D.'s manager, and I run the show when it comes to J.D. Grayling. No one gets to J.D. without going through me."

"Message received loud and clear," I say, ready to shut the door, because the tears are going to come, and I need to get this eye patch off. And more than anything, I'm not going to let this creep see me cry.

CHAPTER SEVEN

These tears are a long time coming from this tense day. I don't know why I thought any of this would be easy. Maybe I shouldn't even be here, but then what choice did I have? Okay, wash my face, get my composure back, and go check the instruments. But first I should probably get something to eat. This shakiness is most likely low blood sugar along with a side of humiliation. At least I can blame it on that. I think I'll skip the big shin-dig buffet and get something little at the café on the lower level. My quick perusal of the eating options before Mr. Rude showed up is coming in handy right now. Plus, I'm not ready for the stares in the big dining room, and there are probably a lot of tourists going to the buffet lunch. And that's it, I am losing the veil and going with the patch only. What will be, will be. How many times did I hear mom say that when she knew we were painted in a corner over something? I've always had stares so why would this place be any different? I guess lilacs, horses, and fresh breezes from the Straits don't change human nature. Too many thoughts, and I have a job to do. A sandwich, a cup of coffee, and then to my instruments.

What a cute little menu and café! I love these wicker chairs, wicker tables, and the big black and white checkered floor in the long hall that runs on this lower floor of the Grand. Ambiance! All these people walking by on their way down to the shops further on down the hall, pause and sneak a glimpse at the beautiful way the Grand serves the little lunches. I'm doing the same thing and I don't mind this wait. I see someone has something that looks delicious. A grilled cheese, a cup of tomato soup, and coffee. Yes, that sounds good—the perfect comfort food lunch. I didn't know tomato soup was possible beyond the red and white can, but I'm sure this version will be homemade. So far so good.

Ah, my turn! Seems like I just sat down, and here's my waiter.

"What would you like today, milady?" he asks while setting down my water served in a beautiful goblet with the Grand logo of the horse and carriage in red on the glass.

"I'll have the lunch special please, the grilled cheese and soup, and a cup of coffee."

"Sounds good, I'm sure you'll love it. No one makes tomato soup like our chefs. Cream for the coffee?"

"Yes, please."

"Right away, milady."

Where else in the world do you get called milady except in a Victorian novel? It makes me feel … what's the word …? Sunshiny inside. Yes, sunshiny.

"You must be Alice."

"Oh, I'm sorry I was daydreaming. Do I know you?" I ask this tall, handsome redhead.

"No, you don't know me, but you met my wife Piper on the boat this morning, and she said to see if I saw you around the hotel today. I'm Cam Nelson."

"Yes, she did say you had red hair. Oh sorry, I'm sure you already know that," I say.

"No problem, and she did tell me I could find you because you are wearing an eye patch. I hope you don't find me too forward, but it was an easy way to find you with all these people starting to pour in."

"Yes, I'm pretty unique that way I guess, not easy to miss."

"Well, it let me find you, and I'm happy I did. Piper was hoping you would join us for dinner this evening at our cottage. You can't miss it. Head to the end of the porch that opens up. We have a big flag out front with lilacs on it. I know it's last minute; we understand if you can't make it. It would be great if you could join us," Cam says.

"Actually, that would be so nice. I was a little nervous about hitting the big hall for dinner tonight, and I would enjoy the company. What time should I arrive?"

"If you can come at 6:30, that would be perfect. Do you like most foods, or is there something you can't have because of allergies? We've learned to ask that after an incident with peanuts."

"Wise move! That's very considerate. I'm allergic to tea of all things, so I don't drink tea, but it's not much of an issue because most people don't cook with it. Silly, huh? I like anything, and please don't fuss over me. Peanut butter and jelly sandwiches would work fine for me, really. I'm not picky."

"Ha! I think we can do a little better than that, and best we get you before you become too used to what meals you are going to be experiencing at the Grand. They will blow you away. My wife says I make a mean pizza if that's okay?"

"Pizza sounds wonderful."

"Milady, I have your lunch." The waiter has arrived with my food.

"Hey Tommy, how are you doing?" Cam asks the waiter.

"Excellent Cam, and you?"

"Doing well. Beautiful day. Listen Alice, I'm gonna run and let you eat, but we'll see you at 6:30, and you have our number in case anything comes up?" Cam asks.

"Yes, I do. I'll see you then. And thank you, really, thank you," I say.

"Our pleasure. Bye, Alice. See yah, Tommy," Cam says as he runs off.

"Mr. Cam is a great guy. Well, here is your sandwich, soup, and coffee. Sorry I didn't bring it out sooner. I saw you were busy," Tommy says.

"No problem. It all looks so delicious," I say. "Thank you."

"I'll check back with you shortly to see if you need anything else. Enjoy!"

And off he goes. How nice to hear my waiter say Cam is a great guy. I'm so thankful to have the chance to avoid the main dining room for this first night and not run into Montague Cheshire.

Ugh. Speak of the devil. There he goes down the hall into what looks like a men's store. I hope he didn't see me when he walked by. Probably not, so self-absorbed he doesn't see the world around him. I'll be finished eating before he comes by, and I can avoid him again – my new goal in life. So, I think I just sign my name on this bill, and it says there's no tipping. That makes this all amazingly easy, especially for me with my food included in my deal. As much of a scoundrel as Uncle Rabbit is, he sure did me a favor when it came to this set-up.

Okay. Time to see if my precious instruments arrived unscathed. So, according to the map, back down the hall, up the stairs, to the left, up the other stairs, down the hall filled with pictures on every available space, and down to the right. There it is. The concert hall where J.D. will be performing. Oh my! This is magnificent and the loudest walls I've ever seen! Stripes in pink and white are not the norm for a hall, but here at the Grand, they go all out, and it always works!

There it is — the room off the stage. That's going to be my new office. It's nice no one is around. I won't be bothered when I look over the instruments. On the other hand, with no one around, someone could get to my instruments very easily. I think I'll have to ask about security for the instruments. I see the door up ahead. I wonder if it's locked. Hmm, no one gave me a key. I'll have to go back to the check-in desk and ask about that if it's not open.

"Can I help you, miss?" Wow. What a deep voice, and there I go again, feeling like I'm jumping out of my skin. When will I learn to pay attention to my surroundings?

"Sorry, I didn't see anyone. Yes, I'm here as the tech for the instruments, and I believe that room next to the green room by the stage is where they have been put, but I wasn't given a key. I would hope it would be locked, for safety, that kind of thing."

"That's the music room. Are you Alice Merveille?" he asks.

"Yes, that's me. And you are?" I ask.

"I'm Joe. I'm the custodian in charge of this area of the Grand. I had a note that you would be coming. I actually have your key for the door. Only a few of us have a key, so please take care of it," Joe says as I follow him to the door. "We don't have a theft problem here, but we don't want to have one either if you get my drift. It should be locked. That's what was supposed to happen after the delivery, you know, standard procedure."

"Makes sense. I'll take the key if you don't mind. I'm rather anxious to see if everything arrived okay and is intact."

"Sure, here you go. I think it's all good. I wasn't here when it was delivered, but we are used to being careful with things," Joe says, handing me the key as we get up close to the door.

"Well, here we go. It is … wait. It's ajar. The door isn't closed. Did you think it was locked?"

"Yes, it should have been locked. Push the door open. Maybe someone forgot," he says.

Why do I feel nervous to push open a door? Here I go. What do we have? Let's see. Two drum kits — check. Two electric guitars — check. Two twelve strings — check. Three acoustic guitars — check. Two bass guitars — check. Two keyboards —

check. Two mandolins — check. Two violins — check. One cello -— check. All the sound equipment. It's all here. Everything looks good. But wait. Where's my guitar? It should be here with all the guitars for the band. Let's see, if I push the sound equipment back and the guitars to the side—no, I'm not seeing it. I don't like this. I love my guitar.

"Everything look, okay?" Joe asks.

"Yes, it all seems to be here, except I'm missing something very dear to me, my own personal guitar that I've had for years. It should be here with the rest."

"Hmm. You're sure you sent it with everything and didn't have that delivered to your room?" he asks.

"No, it was with all the other instruments. It has to be here," I say. What am I missing? It has to be here.

"Uh-oh. I think this is what you're looking for," Joe says as he pushes the door back so we can see behind the inside of the door.

"You found it? Why would it be away from everything else. Wait, you said uh-oh."

"Because someone messed with it. It's smashed to smithereens, and it's been thrown behind this door," he says holding up the neck which is no longer a part of the guitar.

My heart is breaking. One of the few things I have that my mom gave me. I've treasured it from the Christmas morning when I saw it gleaming under our tiny tree. This is not fixable. There are too many small pieces. It's like someone hit it over and over again. With all my stickers on the case, it was pretty obvious this wasn't one of the new instruments with the group.

"Someone had to open the guitar case, take it out, smash it, and then hide it. I'm confused why they wouldn't just steal it for themselves—why they didn't sell it instead of destroying it and then hiding it behind this door?" I ask.

"That's a shame. I'm sorry to see that. Like I said, we don't normally have those kinds of problems here," Joe says.

I don't dare say what I'm thinking out loud. I'll tell you why, Joe. I think it's been left here for me to see. Someone is leaving me a message. I don't know anyone here. Who would do such a thing? There's no way ... he can't be that immature!

CHAPTER EIGHT

I hope I did the right thing by talking Joe out of going to the police to file a report. I don't suspect him. This is not how I want to start my time here, and I know who did it. It's Montague's way of getting back at me. I guess this answers the question rolling around in my mind if he's a man or a disgruntled teenage boy. It's pretty clear he's not a mature man. I'm not letting this go by. He better have an answer for me. My turn to pound on his door.

"Who is it?" he uses the saccharine sweet voice when he's not sure who is knocking.

"It's Alice Merveille."

"Oh, I'll be right there." Again, the tone change when he knows it's me.

"I think we can keep our meeting to the upcoming daily meeting. I'll be getting you a schedule where you can ask any questions you have at that time," he says, rolling his eyes.

"Yes, that will work just fine, but it won't answer the one burning question I have right now after examining the equipment."

"Oh, and what would that be?"

"Why did you take my personal guitar and smash it all up and hide it behind the door?"

I'm watching your face, mister.

"What are you talking about? I didn't touch your guitar or any of the instruments. I didn't even go to the music room yet."

"Interesting because Joe, the maintenance man, told me there are only a few keys. He has one. I have one. J.D. will have one, and you have one. Since I just met Joe, I don't think he has a vendetta against me, and you've made it clear you do. So that puts you as the prime suspect for wrecking my guitar."

I hope he senses the sparks flying from my eye.

"I'm sorry to hear your guitar was damaged, but I had nothing to do with it, and I resent the tone you are using with me!"

"Really? You had a key, and you've treated me nothing but poorly since we met. The guitar was clearly my personal item, and you had nothing to do with it? Perhaps you didn't do the deed yourself, but did you hire someone to take care of it for you?" I ask.

"Listen missy, I didn't know your guitar was here. I didn't hire someone to touch it, and I haven't been to that room yet, so stop the accusations. I don't like you, and you don't like me, but that doesn't mean I would attack your personal possessions. I didn't do it. How much clearer can I be?"

As his voice is getting louder and louder, several people are sticking their heads out in the hall to see what is causing the ruckus. In his usual pattern, I'm noticing his need to make sure people think well of him if they don't know him. To cover up for those watching, he mutters a small apology for the noise and yanks me inside his room.

"There, now you've made a spectacle. Is there any end to the trouble you cause? You better be as good a tech as they say, or you'll be out on your ear within the week. And to say the least, you are on probation."

"You seemed ..."

"I'm not finished! For the last time, I didn't wreck your guitar, and I don't know who did. I suggest you take it up with the police and make sure the other instruments are safe for when J.D. arrives. This will be our last conversation until the group meeting, and as I said, you are on probation."

As he opens the door, he grabs my arm again, shoves me out in the hall, and shuts the door. This guy is the worst. But, ugh! I don't think he did it. I have no choice but to believe him at this point. Great. Now I have an unknown new enemy who wants to hurt me, no guitar, and my boss is waiting for me to make one more wrong move before he fires me. And I did this all on my first day. I thought getting rid of Uncle Rabbit would solve a lot of my problems, but it seems wherever I go, there they are. Maybe I should have reported it to the island police. I don't know. I'll ask Piper and Cam at dinner. I need advice from someone other than myself. The problem is, I don't have a long list of "someones." That's even sadder than a lost guitar.

CHAPTER NINE

There it is — the cottage right past the porch of the Grand with the big lilac flag. Cam's right. I couldn't miss it. Cute little wraparound porch and darling little horse knocker.

"Alice, you're here! Welcome. Come on into our humble abode," Cam says.

"Piper, Alice is here," he yells toward the next room. "Did you have any trouble finding it?"

"No, not at all. Right here where you said it would be with the big lilac flag. Easy to find."

"Alice, welcome! I'm so glad this worked out for you to come to dinner. I should have asked you this morning on the boat. I was so happy when Cam was able to find you and give you the message. Dinner will be ready in a minute. Cam is playing homemade pizza chef tonight, so we have a minute to visit. So how was your first day?" Piper asks, motioning me to join her on the couch. I've never met someone so full of words!

"Well, the Grand is beautiful, just as I remembered when I saw it from the outside as a school kid. My room is amazing with a pink theme. And there's a good chance I'm going to get fired before my job even begins," I say.

"Yes, the Grand is … wait … what? Fired from being the music tech?" Piper

"Ladies, here is some sparkling cranberry juice to hold you over for the next few minutes while the pizza is cooking," Cam says entering the room with juice in champagne flutes.

"Thanks honey," Piper says. "Sit down a minute. Alice is having a day, and maybe we can help."

"Oh, I'm sorry to hear that. What's happening?" Cam asks.

"I'm sorry to burden you right away, but I do need your advice. I've already had some rough words with J.D Grayling's manager who has a very abrasive personality and didn't like me from the moment we met. He made that clear with remarks about my face," I say.

"What? He made rude remarks about your face? Are you kidding me?" Piper asks.

"Well, to be fair, I gave him a piece of my mind right off the bat, and we've sparred ever since in the few times our paths crossed. Here's the kicker. When I went to examine the instruments that arrived from my uncle's shop, they were all fine except for my personal guitar. It was smashed beyond repair and thrown behind the door," I say.

"Oh, that's horrible! I'm so sorry to hear that," Cam says. "We don't usually have problems like that with deliveries at the Grand. It's a pretty well-run, safe place."

"That is terrible, Alice. Your new boss did this to you?" Piper asks. "That's abusive and shouldn't be allowed for sure!"

"Well, since me, the custodial person, and this manager are the only ones who have keys to that room, he seemed the obvious choice," I say.

"You mean Joe, right?" Cam asks.

"Yes, he was the one who came in when I entered the hall before I got close to the room which I thought would be locked, but the door was slightly open," I say.

"I've known Joe for years, and he's a good, solid guy. He

would never do anything like that, I mean if you were wondering about him," Cam says.

"Honestly, I came to that conclusion right off the bat. With Montague — did I mention that's his name, Montague Cheshire? He was the obvious choice. I went and confronted him this afternoon," I say.

"Oh, gutsy, Alice," Piper says.

"I'm trying to be that person, you know, bolder. I've been rather mousey these past few years—who am I kidding—my whole life. I'm hoping this fresh island air and atmosphere can help me improve. It's not my nature, but I'm trying to step up and not be a doormat, since, well, today," I say.

"What happened when you confronted him?" Cam asks.

"He denied it, vehemently, and said he hasn't even been to the room," I say.

"And you believe him?" Piper asks.

"The problem is, even though he's a jerk, I do believe him. No one is that good of a liar, at least I hope not," I say. "Joe wanted me to report it to the police, but I talked him out of it, and I guess that's what I'm wondering from you both. Should I report it to the police?"

"I don't think it would hurt to 'file a report' as they say, in case there is some kind of pattern. What do you think, Cam?" Piper asks.

"I agree with the way you're thinking, Piper. Is it possible the delivery people broke it and tried to hide it?" Cam asks. "They aren't always island people."

"I brought that up to Joe. He said there are forms that are signed against what is on list of deliveries, and it shows they were all there safe and sound. He recognized the names. The only explanation is that someone got into the room after the safe delivery and broke it. I mean, maybe someone did it by accident, and it's not this big conspiracy. That's why I'm very hesitant to bring the police in. It's a big deal to me because my mom gave me the guitar, but it's not a big deal in the grand scheme of things. All the other instruments are of far greater value and resalable. I'm leaning toward chalking it up to some kind of freak thing and letting it go for now," I say. "I've already caused problems, and it's not been a smart way to start my time here."

"I can see that viewpoint, too. If you call the police, then they have to do a report, start an investigation …" Cam says.

"And, with you being so new to this employer, I can see where it looks like you are causing trouble when you've already had a run in with your new boss. I can see value in waiting too; but meanwhile, you don't have your guitar. That stinks," Piper adds.

"It's more the sentiment that bothers me. There are several acoustic guitars, and I'll be bringing things to my room off and on I'm sure for tuning purposes, so, if I want to play, I will have access to one. You know, the more we're talking this out, the more I'm inclined to 'wait and see'. I think I needed to talk it through with someone other than myself. And besides, we have talked enough about me and my guitar fiasco. I want to hear more about you two," I say. "I didn't mean to plop down on your couch and monopolize the conversation."

"Not at all. I'm glad we could help, if we did, I mean. That's quite an incident to encounter on your first day here. Hey, I hear a timer ding, so the pizza is ready. I'm going to get that on the table if you two ladies would arrive at the dining table in about two minutes; everything will be all set," Cam says, heading for the kitchen.

"Are you really busy tomorrow Alice?" Piper asks, moving closer to me on the couch.

"I'm going to go over the instruments, but otherwise, I'm pretty free. The entourage and J.D. aren't here for a few days yet, so these next few days are probably the freest I'll have in a while."

"Before I forget to mention it, I want to invite you to come down to our shop tomorrow, anytime really. I want you to meet Freddy, who is like an uncle to me and lives above the store. He came here from San Francisco, where I'm from. We wouldn't be able to do all we do without his help," she says with the biggest smile.

"But Piper … this is awkward. My face — you probably have a lot of people in the store and believe me, as you saw, they get weird around me. They stare and make comments and …"

"No, that has got to be put behind you. You have to start living, girl! Sometime, when we have time, I want to hear all about your past. It sounds like it has not been an easy journey you have been on. I can relate. What you see here in a cottage with Mr. Wonderful, believe me, that was not my life, at all. I started to look forward instead of looking back and things changed. I met God and my life changed. What do you think about God and His Son, Jesus?" she asks.

Whoa. God? I can't believe she asked me that!

"God? Umm," I say.

Wait a minute. Have I just stumbled into one of those religious things where people knock, barge in, and leave a pamphlet? Am I about to get a pamphlet-type spiel in person? Maybe this is why she's being so nice. Some kind of newbie indoctrination is about to happen. Yikes! I'm so naïve. What have I just stepped into?

CHAPTER TEN

"L adies! Dinner is served!" Cam is calling us to the table. Talk about being saved by the bell.

"We'll talk more later. I can tell by your face I scared the dickens out of you, and that was not my intent. Believe me, I've been in your shoes on that one, too. I'm not some religious nut, so please keep an open mind. This is just a meal and a chat with no strings attached," Piper says as we make our way into the dining room.

"I'm going to be honest, I thought maybe you were going to give me a pamphlet or something," I say, glancing to the side to see her expression at my honesty.

"Oh, thank you for your sense of humor! Alice, I'm the real deal about everything, including my faith. If you don't want to talk about it, I understand. I get pretty excited about how my life has changed for the better. I've been known to bulldoze people. I have to get better at that. It worked for my friend, Sister Mary-Margaret. She was direct with me. I didn't mean to scare you, so another lesson learned, really. We're cool. We can talk about anything that makes you comfortable," she says hesitating for a moment and then adding, "I just sensed I have something you need."

As the delicious aroma of pizza hits me, I realize how hungry I am. Probably best not to answer. *Just move toward the table, Alice. Take your seat and comment on something else. But, still, she's not far off about me needing a lot.*

"The pizza smells amazing. I really am hungry," I say.

"Don't tell me. Piper Penn just rolled over you with an earth-shattering deep question you weren't ready for?" Cam asks, putting a big juicy slice of pizza on my plate.

"Well, kind of … And you have salad, too? Cam, you discovered my favorite meal without asking!" I say.

Please, let's talk about something else before any more weirdness arises between me and these nice people who have invited me so graciously into their home.

"We're good, honey. I did bulldoze her, and I'm so sorry, Alice. Cam, you know me. I'm subject to bursts of enthusiasm as my husband here likes to remind me," Piper says with a wink at me and Cam.

They are so adorable, and free. She is authentic. It's possible I took her the wrong way.

"Not to make you feel even funnier, but we do pray before we eat, Alice, which you may or may not do, I'm not sure. Do you mind if we do?" Cam asks.

"Oh my, not at all. I'm not used to it, but seems like a perfectly good idea," I say, bowing my head.

"Dear Lord, thank you for this day, this food, and for our new friend, Alice. God, please make it clear who wrecked her guitar and get her a new one. Please help Alice to feel comfortable and happy in her new home and new position. And Lord, please help Piper not to chase her off with enthusiasm, which she is subject in frequent bursts of at any moment of the day. In Jesus's name, amen." Cam says.

I look up and see the smile on both of their faces, and we all bust out laughing!

"That is one of the most interesting prayers I've ever heard, even though I've heard very few in my life. Do you really talk to

God about everything, not just world peace and wars and things?" I ask.

All of a sudden, I really don't care if we change the subject. It feels good to have an honest conversation with genuinely nice people. What do I know? I'm too used to pushing people away.

"Since you asked, yes, Jesus is a friend that sticks closer than a brother it says in the Bible. We talk to Him just like we talk with you. Nothing is off limits. Have you read the Bible at all?" Piper asks. "Please tell me if I'm overstepping my boundaries again."

"No, it's fine. I haven't read the Bible, but it's funny you say that. When my uncle took some boxes to a thrift store in Cheboygan, they gave him a Bible and he gave it to me. They said it was a modern language Bible, so I brought it along. I haven't looked at it though."

"Well, try starting out with reading a book in the Bible called John. That's a good one to begin with," Cam says passing me the pickle tray.

"Thank you. This is all delicious by the way. Best pizza ever," I say. "Honestly, I've never given much thought to the Bible or religion in general. My mom never talked about it and beyond an occasional funeral, it just hasn't been on my radar. The preacher read some verses at my mom's funeral — 'The Lord is my Shepherd.' I've heard that one. That's about it."

"You sound like us before we met and as we were both getting to know each other a few years ago here on the island. Although Cam was new to it too, I grew up with a pastor dad who didn't live up to anything he was teaching. I knew a lot about the Bible and Christianity, but I rejected it, big time," Piper says. "It was my friendship with Sister Mary-Margaret and her inviting me to read the book of John that really got me thinking about a relationship with Jesus for myself. I have a lot to learn, but now I know He is my friend. He came to die for my sins, and nothing can separate me from His love," Piper says.

"A real relationship changed everything for Piper and me.

We don't think the same. We look to the Lord for direction in our lives, and He's the basis for our marriage. It's all different than it would be if we didn't know Him. That's why Piper is so enthusiastic. She knows life without Him as her friend and Lord and she knows life with Him. With Him doesn't compare to before," Cam says. "Now we have this peace … this assurance … even when the circumstances in our lives aren't easy. And, let's face it, very few people have an easy life."

"That's really it, Alice. We're not weirdos. We're not selling you anything. We just love to talk about the best thing in our lives, because someone took the time to talk to us. And please don't think that's why I invited you to dinner. We just want to be friends. Sister Mary-Margaret always let me talk about God as much or as little as I wanted to, and I want to do the same for you. You might find this highly interesting, or you may be ready to run for the door. Either way, we simply want to be friends and have some fun while you're here," Piper says.

"Thank you. Really, thank you. I'm not used to anyone taking this much interest in me. I don't remember much about my dad. My mom passed from cancer, and until this week, I've lived with an uncle who wasn't even a blood relative. He is not a nice person, so this trip here is my first step out into the world alone to try to understand where I fit in. So far, it hasn't felt like I do fit anywhere, but you've made me feel comfortable. I'm not just saying that. You are both so genuinely, well, kind," I say.

"Not to sound crass, but what you just said makes you a part of our club — the orphan club. My parents have passed, so has Cam's; Freddy's of course, Sister Mary-Margaret …We've all known that pain and that grief that you don't get until it happens to you," Piper says.

"My goodness. It's true! Someone who hasn't been through it, doesn't totally get what the loss and longing are like. I'm sorry for your loss, and thank you for telling me," I say.

"Of course, we don't want to make light of anyone's parent passing, but we've all found a kinship in helping each other deal with it because we've all 'walked a mile in those shoes' as the old adage goes. It's a weird club, but it's a helpful club," Cam adds.

"I'm happy I met you today. I'm truly not signing you up for some multi-level marketing deal; although, yeah, I can see how you might think that. Between all the fun at the shop and getting to hear some music from J.D. Grayling—this could be a rockin' fun summer! I love his music. I've worn out his cassettes," Piper says. "Oh, how about 'Light' and 'Raincheck'… wait … will you be playing with him too?"

"Not really, I don't think so. It would have to be a dire situation for them to need me to fill in. I know the music and I could. But they don't know me, and they may not even realize I can play all his music. Besides, I might get with all these professional musicians and find out I'm nothing more than a puffed-up amateur. I was contracted to be the music tech, to keep the instruments in tip-top shape, switch them out between songs as needed, and that sort of thing. Who knows what will be happening after the run in with Mr. Cheshire?" I say.

"Wait, your name is Alice, and he's Mr. Cheshire, it's like …" Cam says.

"Yes…strange, huh? *Alice in Wonderland*. And for what the summer holds, I'm not sure how many rabbit holes I'll be going down with him as my boss. I plan on laying low, doing my job, and staying out of his way as much as I can. I'm hoping when he sees I am good at being a music tech, he will be nicer around me. We'll see," I say.

"I know you just got here, but have you by any chance run into the Mackinac Island Town Chairwoman Katherine Sims-Dubois, yet?" Piper asks.

"Oh, please Piper, the lady has had a hard enough day as it is," Cam says.

"Come on Cam. We are being forgiving, kind people, remember?" Piper says. "I'm just warning you because she is quite overpowering, a 'real force' as some townspeople say. She swoops in on new people at the Grand and makes it clear she runs the town and the world. I mean, I should talk, because look at me. I kind of 'swooped' on you, too. But if you're talking about the story of Alice, um, she would have the role of the Queen of Hearts," Piper says with a giggle.

"Off with their heads!" Cam yells and makes a swinging motion.

"Cameron Raymond Nelson!" Piper says, clearly trying to hold back a laugh. "You have to be better than me. She's a sore spot, Alice, because they are relatives. You talked about an uncle that's a problem — she's his continual problem."

"It's almost scary to hear about her. Will I have to interact with her in my role?" I ask.

"Probably not, but she's one of those people who says whatever she wants. She perceives herself as some kind of queen of the island. She knows who lives here and who doesn't. Brace yourself, because with your eye patch, she may make some grand gesture or inquire about it in a way that, knowing her, might be inappropriate. Oh man, I'm making this sound like a bigger deal than I should. Ah, maybe I shouldn't have brought it up," Piper says. "I think instead of reminding Cam, I should go look in the mirror."

"She wears crazy skirts and shoes with flowers painted on them and big hats and …." Cam says.

"And be assured she will seek out J.D. because of his fame. I think it's okay that I'm warning you, because too many times I've seen her throw people for a loop. This way, you won't be caught off guard. We are trying to think kindly of her. It's just not easy with the weekly run-ins we experience. Katherine Sims-Dubois is all about Katherine Sims-Dubois if you get my drift," Piper says amplifying her voice in a way that must sound like Katherine. "And we are the worst people in the world talking like this. Seriously, Alice, forgive us. Just don't be afraid of her. She's harmless, but loud," Piper says throwing her arms up and shrugging her shoulders.

"Just watch the show when it happens, have a good laugh,

and don't give her a second thought, no matter what she says," Cam says. "She doesn't wield the power she thinks she does, so we don't want you to be taken in with her bravado."

"Now, I kind of can't wait to meet her," I say suddenly finding all this pretty amusing.

"That's it," Piper says. "Again, we are not trying to be unkind, but she's put us through a lot. We are always reminding ourselves to take the high road — to act like people who follow Jesus and practice kindness and love in our lives. She's a constant test for us."

"When do you think I might see this 'Katherine show' come my way?" I ask.

"Let's see, you've been here one day, so I would predict in the next day or two if you are around. All the more reason to come hang out at our shop tomorrow. She doesn't show her face there very much. I think deep down, she's afraid of Freddy. He's put her in her place a few times, and she doesn't like that at all," Piper says.

"What kind of crazy island have I wandered onto here for the summer, Mr. and Mrs. Nelson? Sounds like a Jesus-loving, skirt-swooshing, guitar-wrecking trip down a rabbit hole for sure!" I say.

We all look at each other in a moment of silence and then we lose it. After a good five straight minutes of laughing together, I can hardly catch my breath.

"I better finish this delicious dinner now that I've laughed off about five pounds!" I say.

"And save room for chocolate chip cookies! In fact, let me grab those and get them on the table along with the coffee I brewed," Cam says heading for the kitchen.

"Want to know a secret? He uses Mackinac Island fudge instead of chocolate chips. His cookies are epic! Don't tell him I told you. But, in case you are wondering why they are just out of this world!" Piper says in a whisper.

"Okay, ladies. Here's the next course at Chez Nelson.

Coffee, with cream if you'd like, and my world famous, well, island famous, chocolate chip cookies!" Cam says.

"Eat your heart out chefs at the Grand. I've dined at Chez Nelson," I say. "Okay, one, and only one cookie, and yes, coffee with cream for me, please."

They are so easy to talk to. So easy to laugh with. The evening is flying by, and it is refreshing. Piper has saved me again.

"Well, I better get back and let you two have a little of what's left of the evening. I can't thank you enough for the invitation and the lovely evening. And the pizza, wow! The cookies were wonderful too!" I say. "I know there was something very special about those cookies, but I'd never expect a chef to reveal his secrets, so I won't even ask."

"Hey, we're no Grand Hotel spread, but we won't let you leave hungry," Cam says still chuckling. "Yes, I have a secret, but I must take it to my grave."

"As you should, as all great chefs do," I say winking at Piper.

"Hey, I saw that. Piper, you tell everyone, don't you?" Cam asks.

"You caught me. I think everyone should know you are a genius," Piper says blowing him a kiss. "I'll walk you to the edge of our yard, Alice, and make sure I see you get on the Grand porch. It's very safe here on the island, but no need to be foolish."

"Oh, thank you. Thanks again, Cam. It's been a wonderful evening. I hope to see you soon," I say walking out the door with Piper.

As we cross her yard, I'm seeing the stars for my first night on the island.

"The stars, oh my gosh! They're magnificent! And the moon over the Straits, and oh, the bridge is lit up ... beautiful," I say. This is what awe feels like.

"It never gets old, and it calms me and makes me happy every time I see it all. It is such an awesome sight. You've had a big first day, but I'll be praying that you have a really good second day, and things smooth over with Mr. Grouchy, or as I should respectfully say, Mr. Cheshire. And remember, if you feel a little tug on your heart to open up that new Bible you have, take a look at the book of John. Your story is in there too," Piper says.

"My story? Hmm. There's a girl with a patch and a new friend named Piper?"

"Yes, the girl with a patch and a new friend named Piper. It's all in there. Bye, Alice. Try to come by the shop tomorrow, The Creative Lilac downtown. You can't miss it."

"I will sure try to make it. If I don't, just know it's because I got tied up with work. Otherwise, I will be there. Thanks again for a lovely evening."

"You're more than welcome. Good night," she says with a wave.

"Good night, Piper."

Stepping onto the far end of the porch of the Grand, I realize the people are all dressed up and having their coffee in tiny little cups. It must be a thing to stroll the porch after dinner. This is like what I've seen in the movies — exquisite, elaborate, long dresses and sparkling jewelry. I better get to my room quickly; I'm not fitting in with this crowd wearing my blue jeans. And please, Lord, don't let me run into Montague Cheshire. Please, Lord? Wow, these Jesus-loving people are rubbing off on me. And I'm in the Bible? Come on, Piper! I'm from a small town, I'm admittedly awkward, but I'm not totally gullible. She really wants me to read that book!

What a night. After that nice hot shower, and my head on this pillow for my first night in the Grand Hotel, in my very own room, my brain is racing. It's like a culture shock going from my life with Uncle Rabbit in Cheboygan to being on my own in this one-of-a-kind hotel. But I like some of these new feelings. I feel alive for the first time in a long time, like there's a world out there beyond anything I've ever known. It's exciting and scary at the same time. Even though Uncle Rabbit was usually mean, I was used to it. Meeting a regular person other than behind the music counter at the store is so different and is giving me some kind of courage. It's a courage I didn't know I had. For the first time, I made it through a day without thinking about my disfigured face and eye patch every single minute. That's an accomplishment! There's more to the world than me and my goofy face and eye patch. For a time, this evening, I was just Alice, not Alice with the weird face. Just Alice. She's someone I would like to get to know. Now, if she can only stay employed!

CHAPTER ELEVEN

I like waking up after I've spent the whole night dreaming everything is pink! This room is having an effect on me. Yes, cotton candy does sound good for breakfast. I'll take that over a nightmare anytime. At least I didn't dream about the Cheshire Cat and the Queen of Hearts.

Get going Alice. This is your real life, not a book. Piper and Cam, what a pair. I'm really glad to know them. It feels good to have someone here that isn't related to my music job. If I get up and get going, then I should be able to make it to Piper's shop today. I'll shower, call down for a light breakfast to be brought up — so glad they have that choice — and head down to my music room to do some set up and tuning. I hope everything is as it should be. If it isn't, then I will be going to the police.

Okay. I am a grown-up as proven by my choice of rhubarb jam on an English muffin instead of asking for cotton candy. Out the door I go with my satchel, and yes, my keys, including the music room key — yes, it's all there. My notebook. My sunglasses, affirmative. I should be good for the day. And, if the day warrants sunglasses, that covers up my patch. Then only the bottom of my weirdo face shows. Anything to help with stares. If I time leaving exactly right, I'll be able to peek in the rooms as the maids leave them open while cleaning. So many assorted colors and unique décor. Flowers are a big theme I see along with lighthouses. There's a new one — very distinct-looking cats of assorted sizes. Interesting. I wonder if there's a dog room, too. Okay, through the parlor, up the small stairs, and down the long hall to the big concert hall area. Oh darn, there's a gathering of people right before I can make it in the door. Maybe if I put my head down, and slip by quietly, I can …

"And who in the world are you? My goodness! Is it some sort of 'pirate' themed day that no one told me about? Is this a new fashion statement?" Wow. Now I get it. This has to be the one and only Katherine Sims-Dubois. That is a swishy white shirt with tulips in every color of the rainbow all along the bottom and yes, I can't stop myself from glancing down at her shoes — white pumps with purple tulips on the tips. Tulip earrings and a wide-brimmed lacy hat with, yes, tulips. And one long tulip on her white lacey top.

The people around her swarm like bees with their queen. One thing they all have in common — a look of disdain to match her expression as she stares at me.

"Excuse me, but I don't believe we have met. And you are?" I ask.

"I am Katherine Sims-Dubois, Chairperson of the Mackinac Island Town Council and knowledgeable about all things happening on Mackinac Island, and I do mean *all* things," she says with a nod to her 'hive' who all buzz in agreement. "Do you have authorization to be in this area of the Grand?"

"Why yes, I do, and I'm Alice Merveille by the way. I'm the instrument tech for the upcoming J.D. Grayling shows," I say.

"Well! Why didn't you say you were somebody? A minor somebody, but worth noting I suppose." The hive all nod in agreement. "Are you important enough to say, get me a backstage meeting with J.D., only for the purposes of greeting him as an official island representative, of course. I meet celebrities right and left, so please don't mistake me for some kind of school-girl groupie or something," she says in her rapid fire, old-timey movie accent. "Heaven knows, I have far more important things to do, but I am known as one who never shirks her responsibilities."

"Actually, I'm a peon, a nobody really. You may want to speak with a certain Mr. Montague Cheshire, J.D.'s road manager," I say, looking at the bees to see if anyone is taking a note.

"Write that down Marion. Montague Cheshire." Her crew is falling down on the job. Turning back to me, she narrows her eyebrows once again and gives me a squinty stare.

"Mind you, I have other connections to Mr. Grayling, but I thought since you were here right now, and if you were someone, but clearly, you're … and why exactly are you wearing that patch thing. Do the problems on the bottom of your face extend up into the eye area? Some mishap? Please tell me you have an appointment with a plastic surgeon on your calendar." The hive murmurs.

"I was in an unfortunate accident, and I'm lucky to be alive. Plastic surgery has always been at the bottom of my list. But then I guess my face could always be fixed while your rudeness seems to be a permanent situation that no doctor could possibly tackle."

The hive lets out a collective gasp, her face turns bright red, and I feel extremely proud of thinking up something mean to say to this mean person at this exact moment in time.

"Well! Speaking of rude, you listen to me, young lady…"

"See you, Katherine-Sims DuBois. I have important things to do and talking to you is not one of them."

I'm not hanging around for another collective gasp. *Move fast Alice, through the grand ball doors, unlock the music room, shut it, and wait …. wait.* Nothing. Good. The swarm didn't chase me! I must remember to thank Piper for warning me about this Queen of Hearts, who I will forever now think of as the queen of the hive. I swear most of them were even wearing yellow! She would have devasted me if I hadn't been prepared, but knowing her nature,

I think I did pretty well for myself. Of course, if she's connected to the people at the Grand, this could come back to "sting me."

It is a small island, and everyone probably knows everyone, but I don't care. I'm not here long term. I like this new me with, what's the word … bravado. Yes! I now have bravado, and I like it. I relish the opportunity to call out people who are jerks. Uncle Rabbit, Montague Cheshire, and now Katherine Sims-Dubois. If I were writing a novel, they would all be villains. Thank goodness they are balanced out by nice people — Piper and Cam. Okay, enough. Get to the task at hand. Let's see, I'll do a little organizing in here, getting everything lined up, start a little tuning, and then I should be able to get to The Creative Lilac and see Piper today. Maybe she can set me up with some good paper and pens for doodling, so I have some distractions beside music this summer. That nice little desk area in my room would be a perfect place to sketch the scenery. I'll open a window, let a cool Straits' breeze join me, and relax. Mr. Cheshire made it clear I won't be hanging out with the band, so yeah, that can take up some free time.

I should also hit up the local library and check out some Agatha Christie books I haven't read yet. They're always good for passing the time. Maybe I'll delve back into *Nancy Drew* the way I did in junior high. And, read the book of John in the Bible. Hmm. Maybe. Still not sure about that side of our conversation last night. I've lived this long without religion, although they made a point to say their experience is not about religion, but about relationship. That's a new thought. If God and Jesus are so great, why doesn't everyone automatically believe in Them and reap the rewards? Seems like a no-brainer if it was that perfect. But I really do like Piper and Cam, so I'll have to smile and nod through the faith type stuff. It's worth it to get to hang out with them.

Ahh! Gosh, another knock on my door to make me jump. Please don't be Montague. He wouldn't knock; he'd just barge in. No, it's a woman's voice. Don't be Katherine Sims-Dubois coming after me to get the last word in. Don't be one of her hive on assignment to land the final sting. Please go away. No one should be back here anyway; this is the private music room.

"Yes, can I help you?" I ask, slightly cracking the door so I can slam it fast if necessary.

"Hi, I think you're Alice, and I wanted to introduce myself," she says. "I'm J.D.'s girlfriend Vivian."

"Oh, hello," I say opening up the door. "Yes, I believe Mr. Cheshire mentioned you would be coming with the group," I say. "Are they all here early?"

"Oh no, I'm here now because my uncle owns the Grand Hotel, so I popped in early to see him and my auntie before the guys all get here."

"I didn't know there was a connection to the Grand and the band."

"Actually, yes. This is a much smaller venue for J.D., but I did a little wrangling with my uncle. J.D. needs a nice break and to not work so hard this summer, at least for a few weeks. I knew it would be a great draw to the hotel for my uncle. So voila, I worked my magic and it's happening. I'm glad you could fill in; the regular music tech went out on the road for the summer with a band in Europe, and we weren't sure who could fill in. We've all heard good things about you, and I'm sure you'll do a wonderful job."

"Well, I will do my best. I've never had a gig quite like this, but I have taken many years to perfect tuning all types of instruments and to master being able to restring them quickly. Once I fully understand all that's needed, I'm sure everyone will find my skills adequate," I say.

"Sorry about your face, I mean, something big happened in your life, obviously," she says.

"Yes, a bad accident. The one side of my face, well, it took the brunt of the accident, and my eye isn't highly functional either."

"I just wanted to see who would be working with J.D. this

summer. Believe me, some women just can't wait to get their claws in him, so when I heard you were a girl tech, well, I had to check out everything. Usually we have guy techs."

Oh, okay. She wasn't interested in meeting me; she was making sure I wasn't someone who threatened her relationship with J.D. Still, she seems okay. Exceptionally beautiful, a little snooty too, but not to Katherine Sims-Dubois standards.

"I'm sure you'll meet lots of nice people here this summer and have a fun time. As a band, we kind of keep to ourselves, but the hotel is always teeming with tourists and interesting people."

"I met a very interesting lady when I got here to the grand ball room area, a Katherine-Sims Dubois. She was …"

"Yes! Isn't she the best? I call her Auntie Katherine. She's not my relative of course, but she is so important on this island — like one of our inner circles of islanders. Sorry I missed her. We haven't had a chance to connect yet since I arrived, but she is a delight!"

Note to self — read the room before you make a statement about someone who someone else thinks is fabulous.

"Yes, she sure is memorable. What do you do Vivian? It's nice you are able to travel with the band. Do you play and sing?" I ask.

"Oh my no. Can't carry a tune or play a note on anything. I model. Often, I'll pick up a modeling job in the city where J.D. is playing. I actually met him in Paris when I was doing a photo shoot for *Glamour* magazine, and he was on tour. Let's see, six months ago or so now. That's how long we've been together and believe me, that's a lifetime in this business. We are crazy about each other, as I'm sure you've read in the magazines," she says.

I haven't, but okay. I hope she's not going to turn into a fully ripe version of Auntie Katherine as she gets older. Two of them on the island would be too much!

"Sorry, I'm not much of a magazine reader, more books, I guess," I say.

"Well, yes, I guess some people do that. I'll let you get back to your work. I'm sure I'll see you around. I keep pretty close to J.D. That's what he likes, me to be near all the time. Good to see who you are and to know, well , ..."

She trails off not knowing how to finish the sentence after letting out what she is really thinking. Why not just come out and say you are happy to know that I am not a threat to your relationship with J.D.? Lucky me, I passed the test.

"Good to meet you," she says turning to leave." If you need anything from the hotel, like your towels aren't fluffy enough or anything, let me know. Remember I have connections at the top, and I'd be happy to make sure you get what you need. That's just me, always being helpful. Ta ta for now!"

And she's gone. Not exactly who I would see J.D. with. His songs are deep, and she is rather flighty. I would think he'd want more in a companion, but what do I know? I've never met him. The J.D. I think I know, and the real J.D. may be different people. Time will tell, but I hope I'm not disappointed. If I had to make a judgement based on the people he surrounds himself with, I'd say, yikes. But if I make a judgement based on his music, it's wow. So, who is the real J.D.? And can I truthfully admit to myself that meeting his beautiful girlfriend, soon to be fiancé according to Montague made me feel incredibly sad. *Come on Alice. Did you really think you had a chance?*

CHAPTER TWELVE

Walking to Piper's store is an eye opener. Coming here as a kid, I was oblivious to the tourists. I was more wrapped up in my classmate's antics or making sure the teacher didn't see us doing something we shouldn't. This time is different. I see them all now. They flow like fish swimming upstream in every shape, size, color, and speaking in a multitude of languages and accents. And they all come to this little piece of paradise to get away. Everyone seems to like looking in the store windows and watching how fudge is made. Their bags are overflowing with island trinkets to remember their trip. It's a feeling of excitement and happiness wafting in the air like the fragrance of lilacs in full bloom. Even strolling at a leisurely pace, here I am — on the doorstep of The Creative Lilac. Oh, it's so cute! Even this outside decor is a welcoming sight, oozing with personality. Piper's creativity shines and invites island visitors to see what's inside. Cute bell tinkle as I enter, love that, too.

"Welcome to The Creative Lilac. Let me know if I can show you anything in particular or if you just want to browse around. Either way, we're happy you are here." This has to be Freddy — the elderly gentlemen that stays here and helps with the store.

"Thank you. You must be Freddy," I say.

"Why yes, I am, and I'm sorry if we've met and I forgot. My age plays tricks on me sometimes."

"Your memory is fine. We haven't met, but Piper told me about you. I met her recently. I'm Alice."

"Yes, Miss Alice! She told me about meeting you on the ferry and that you had dinner last night. Yes, welcome. I'll let Pip know you are here — she's upstairs." He seems like such a nice man, such a nice smile coming my way as he presses the intercom button. He calls her Pip.

Running down the stairs, Piper is joined by two adorable cats who are seeing if they can beat her to the bottom.

"Hi Alice. I'm so glad you could make it today! You've met Freddy?" she asks.

"Yes, we introduced ourselves, and who are these two rascals?" I ask.

"This is Bijou," she says, pointing to the orangish striped cat. "And this is Labyrinth." The black and white has what almost looks like a star over his one eye.

"Well, look at that. We are peas in a pod, both with eye patches!" I say squatting down near Labyrinth. "I've never had a cat, but I've always wanted cats and a dog. I love them. It never worked out for us to have one. Do they like to be petted?"

"Do they? Non-stop actually. They love people, and our visitors love to pet them as they shop," Freddy says, picking up Labyrinth and handing him to me.

"Oh, Mr. Cuddly, you and I look like each other, but I bet you get less stares and more hugs than I do. Oh sorry," I say, suddenly realizing I'm talking out loud to the cat instead of the people in the room. "Sorry. I got lost in Labyrinth there for a minute," I say. "I'm back now."

"You take all the kitty-cat time you want," Piper says. "We all do it. They are stress-relievers, for sure."

"Your store is amazing! You seem to have a little something for everyone who wants to be creative in any way," I say.

"I'm so glad you think so! That's exactly what we are going

for, something for everyone, because, really, everyone is creative," Piper says.

"How about if you get me started with something simple that I could do at the desk in my room when I'm not working on the instruments. I'm not an artist, but I am a doodler. I like to draw little flowers, guitars, and silly little things. Then I dabble with coloring and painting them. Can I get some paper for sketching, maybe a simple paint set, and let's see … a set of markers to get started?"

"Absolutely! Freddy, why don't you put together what you think Alice needs. I'm going to take her upstairs and show her around and offer her a cold beverage. How does that sound?" Piper asks.

"Sounds like a good plan to me," Freddy says. "I know exactly what you need. You see, I'm an old doodler myself. You girls go have some chitty chatty time."

"Doodle pals! That sounds perfect, Freddy. I appreciate it," I say. He really seems like a character who is always up for fun.

"Thanks, Freddy. Come on, Alice, up this way. Part of upstairs is where Freddy lives, and the other half is storage, a break room type thing and pseudo guest room if it needs to be, too," Piper explains as we head up the stairs. "Have a seat. Would you like a cola, or I have iced tea, or coffee?" she asks as we sit down.

"I'd love a cola, thank you. Seems like you are always serving me something lately. I wish I was giving you something for a change."

"Here you go. Don't be silly. The least I can do is to show you some hospitality," she says.

"This is as fun and lovely up here as it is in your store. There's creativity wherever I look, and I think you mesh with the designer at the Grand. I mean, you put colors and patterns together that the average person would not think of, and just look at this result. It's a feast for the eyes!" I say.

"Ah, thanks for the sweet compliments. It took a little getting used to for Cam. He's the kind of guy that would probably have one picture on the wall, if that. So, it's been an adjustment for him to live with little 'ole artsy me, but true confessions time. I thrive in it, and I don't think I would do well in any other environment. I can't help myself really. Enough about me, did you have a good day so far?"

"Um, a unique day. One you will find interesting. I ran into one certain Katherine Sims-Dubois right outside the grand ballroom at the Grand and thanks to your heads up, I was prepared. I think I would have been very thrown off if you hadn't warned me, so thank you."

"I knew she would be sniffing around. Did you catch that transatlantic accent from the 1930s and 40s movies? Puleeez! I can't quite figure her out. She loves this island, that's for sure, but she has a tough time with anyone on the island who isn't just like her or doing everything she thinks they should. I shouldn't be talking about her, but since you met her for the first time, you may need some … what's the word … help with what you saw," she says breaking out into a giggle.

"That's a good way of putting it. You probably aren't going to like this, but after her comment about my patch and hoping I had an appointment with a plastic surgeon, I did say something snarky, which in hindsight I'm not positive even makes sense, but it felt good at the time."

"Okay, now you know I have to know what you said to her."

"Well, it was along the lines of I can always get plastic surgery but there's no help for how you treat people, or something like that. I don't remember exactly. Her whole hive — that's what I call her entourage that was with her, buzzing around like she was a queen bee — the whole hive gasped. She wanted to know if I could get her backstage to personally greet J.D, but then she concluded that since I wasn't that big of a somebody, she would use some other connections she had. I'm not sure if I'm even remembering it all. I felt good afterward and quickly escaped to my music room before she could say anything else."

"Whoa … the queen of hearts, am I right? But yes, I like your queen bee analogy too, very spot on. Oh, I'm trying so hard to be more loving, but she makes it really hard! That's the kind of nasty things she does if she ever shows up here, which isn't very often, thankfully. And Cam, he has known her and put up with her most of his life. He struggles with his feelings, knowing we are to love our enemies and pray for those who persecute us. That's what Jesus said, and we know that's what we should be doing, but we often fail," she says.

"It sounds good in theory I suppose, but it felt really good to give it back to her. I've spent most of my life biting my tongue, and as weird as it is, since I've been here, I've stood up to first Mr. Cheshire, and now her. Like it's not even me! I wish I would have had this kind of boldness with my uncle."

"I hear you; it feels really good in the moment. But, in my experience, giving into that moment leads to all kinds of bad feelings in the aftermath. I've had to learn my old nature likes instant gratification, but I don't do myself any favors in the long run. Honestly, I do hear you. She had it coming. But then, maybe I should have kept my mouth shut and not put any ideas in your head. I felt bad about that after you left. I remember the ways she has rolled over me, and I wanted to protect you from what she can inflict on unsuspecting victims."

"Don't feel that way. I was glad to be prepared. I think I have to find the happy medium between not being a doormat but not lashing out. Stuffing my feelings for so many years doesn't mean I should say whatever I want to anyone. It's like someone shook up this can of cola for many, many years and then opened the top to an explosion!"

It is so easy to talk to Piper, like I've known her for years. I don't remember it ever being this easy to talk to anyone.

"Believe me, you wouldn't have liked the former Piper very much if you met her before I understood my need for a personal relationship with Jesus. I exploded constantly, daily in fact. She resurfaces way more than I would like, but I'm working on her. With God's help, I'm improving," Piper says, turning to look out the window a moment. "Has anyone ever told you about the Bible verse, John 3:16?"

"Um, my true confession time. I didn't have the time to read the book of John as you suggested. I'll probably get to it …"

"Don't worry. You have been on the island for like two minutes. That verse says that God loved the world so much He gave His only Son, and that whoever believes in Him will not perish, but have eternal life," Piper says.

"So, escape hell and go to Heaven, is that it? It sounds really stupid to say this in front of you, but I have never given much thought to any of it. You know I didn't go to church at all growing up, and none of my friends ever talked about God. I mean, I know there is a God, and when my mom passed from cancer, I may have thought about it a little, but not long. I don't even know if I want to think about it. I've tried to be a good person, well, until I got here and started exploding at everyone. So, maybe I'm good enough to make it? I've never committed a crime or killed anyone or anything. I don't think I'm important enough for God to worry about. He's got wars, and world hunger, and peace on his plate."

"Here's my Bible. Let's look at the verse one more time, but this time, let's put your name in there. For God so loved the world He gave his only Son, that if Alice believes in Him, she will not perish, but have eternal life," she says.

"How is that possible?"

"It says 'whosoever', so that means absolutely everyone who believes in Him will have eternal life," she says.

"It's got to be more difficult than that."

"It's not. It's that simple. Anyone who believes has to be sincere, not just repeat words, but mean it in their heart. Jesus dying on the cross opened up the way for us to have a relationship once again with God. That friendship was severed when sin entered the world. God and sin can't coexist. And we wouldn't want it to — we are looking forward to a world that has no sin. You know what it's like if you put even one drop of oil in a bucket of water? It's contaminated … it's not pure water anymore. The same thing with God. He's sinless. He can't hang out with sin, but He loves us and wants to be with each and every one of us, His children. So, He sent His Son to die on the cross to take the punishment that we deserved. Now, when we come to the Father, he doesn't see sinful you and me anymore, He sees Jesus, and Jesus steps up and says, this is another one I died for. But that's only true for anyone who accepts His free gift of salvation. He offers it to everyone."

I've never heard anything like this in my life! I had no idea this was in the Bible, that way I mean. I thought it was a bunch of old stories that didn't really apply to me. It's mind boggling to hear Piper talk to me about this.

"Are you staying with me here? I can't tell by the look on your face," Piper says.

"Yes. If I look shocked, it's because, why don't I know this," I say.

"Let's look at the next verse, John 3: 17 — 'For God did not send his Son into the world to condemn the world, but to save the world through Him'," she says.

"So, Jesus died on the cross to save me from my sins, and to make it okay for me and God again, is that right?" I ask.

"Yes, He died for anyone who will believe what He says happened, that He rose again, and that He wants a relationship, including guiding the life you have on earth."

"So, why doesn't everyone just believe it? Why isn't it more well-known or common knowledge? Why aren't church people out knocking on doors telling people this?" I ask.

I know my voice is going up in volume, but really, what is the deal with this kind of news and people not knowing it?

"Because, in the process, we are asked to make Jesus The Lord of our lives. To put into practice what He taught us in the

Bible. To do the hard things which means a lot of dying to yourself. The old nature, the before we ask Jesus to take over the person we were, wants to satisfy self. It's not easy. Think of any toddler you've ever seen in a store that wants a toy and throws a fit when they don't get it. That's how you and I feel when we want what we want, and maybe that isn't the plan God has for our lives. It all becomes about His ways and Him. Not everyone is willing to do that."

"So, there's a little more to the story than a free trip to Heaven. There's a catch."

"Not a catch, but a reality that He does want us to live the way He instructs us to in the Bible. When He says, 'Follow Me", He means it. The thing is you don't have to be overwhelmed by all of that. He asks everyone to come as you are right now. The first thing is to accept the free gift of eternal life and decide if you want to believe and follow Him. He works out all the rest with you, personally, like a loving Father. None of us are perfect. We still sin. But it's different. When we sin after giving our hearts to Him, we can talk with Him. We say we're sorry, which is called repenting if you've ever heard that word, and He forgives us. He knows the attitude of our hearts and when we want to change our ways because of our love for Him," she says.

"I can't relate to a father; I mean with my dad gone since I was little. From what I can gather, he treated me like a pest, not his kid."

"Sometime I will tell you more about my past. I can relate to your story. But the truth is, you do have a loving Father — Father God and His Son, Jesus. And when Jesus rose from the dead and then went back up into Heaven after spending thirty-three years here on earth teaching and performing miracles, He sent His Spirit, the Holy Spirit, to comfort and guide us. So, we are never alone! We can always ask God what He wants us to do, and we will always get an answer. He has a plan for each life and a purpose here on earth. Once we accept Him as our Savior, then we are about our Father's business, living out the plan that He prepared for us. We do what Jesus did when He walked the earth — He lived his daily life asking the Father every day what He should do to live out the plan God had for Him. Jesus would have liked to have skipped parts of His earthly life I'm sure, just as any human would — being nailed to a tree and taking on the sins of the world. While Jesus was on earth, He was still fully God, but He was also fully man, experiencing what we experience. The only difference is, He never sinned," Piper says.

"So, Christmas is His coming as a baby and Easter is His dying on a cross," I say.

"Yes, exactly, dying and rising again. Let's look at these verses. Here, I'll turn to the book of Romans. Romans 10:9-10. It says: If you declare with your mouth, 'Jesus is Lord,' and believe in your heart that God raised him from the dead, you will be saved. For it is with your heart that you believe and are justified, and it is with your mouth that you profess your faith and are saved."

"It's as simple as believing it, and I can be saved?" I ask.

"Yes, it's true for you and everyone. Jesus offers us salvation as a free gift, but He doesn't force it on anyone. A gift can be opened or refused. Now you know why I want you to read John, and whatever else you are led to read in the Bible. Opening yourself up to Jesus isn't only about an eternity in Heaven, it's about the life we live here while on earth — it gives life real meaning and purpose," she says.

"Your face lights ups when you talk about it," I say.

"I guess I didn't realize that. It's like … you know this most important, wonderful thing and you want everyone else to at least know about it. I can't make someone see it, but I have to see if they've heard about it at least. Think of this. If I was walking by a burning building, would I try everything in my power to get the people out and save their lives, or would I not want to embarrass myself and keep on walking?"

"Or would you leave it up to the fire department? I mean, can't we leave these types of things up to churches?" I ask.

"That's the thing. Churches are important, but they are buildings. Since we can have Jesus living in us, we, anyone who believes, are the church. And He tells us to tell other people."

"Hmm. That's a new way to look at it," I say.

"I get that it can seem weird or foolish when you first hear about it. The Bible even says that Christianity is foolishness to the unbeliever. But when you do give your heart to Jesus — when you authentically believe—you understand. It's a mystery, hard to explain, but there's a change. You see it differently. It's funny because I grew up with a pastor dad who was very much a hypocrite. As time went on, he started to treat being a Christian like a business. It got worse when he became a celebrity preacher on TV. I never understood how personal it is and how important it is that I understand in my heart and soul what Jesus did when He chose to follow His Father and go to the cross. Even in the garden of Gethsemane where He was praying the night before He was taken to the cross, He asked His Father if this cup could pass from Him. In other words, He was asking if there was another way to save humanity. He knew a horrifying death was about to happen. But He did it anyway out of His great love for each of us. It blows me away really. No one, not even Cam, has ever loved me that much," Piper says.

Seeing the tears in her eyes, I feel them coming in mine, too. I had never heard this, known this, or understood so much about Jesus. I haven't given Him two thoughts, not even when I would see a cross on a church or hanging on someone's wall.

"My mind is getting blown right now, too, Piper. I haven't had a lot of deep talks with anyone since my mom passed, and never about this kind of thing. So, how do you do it? Do you go to church and sign up?" I ask.

"Going to church is great, because that's how you grow, but really, it's just a prayer from you to Him that you know you are a sinner, you want forgiveness, and yes, you believe in Him. You acknowledge that He did this all for you. That's all there is to it. When you say that prayer in your own earnest way, He hears and accepts it. It says in the Bible that your name is written in the Lamb's Book of Life, and you are His child forever and ever."

"Is it really that simple, that's what you do?"

"Yes, but it's not a simple road to walk, because your life isn't all about you anymore. Instead, it's about Him, the Father, and the Holy Spirit," she says. "You have to count the cost of what you are deciding. Now, instead of doing what feels easy or right to you, you are called as His child to follow what He teaches us in His word and through His Spirit. But you don't have to do it in your own strength — you have the Holy Spirit. And that's another big mystery that's hard to wrap your mind around — how the Father, the Son, and the Holy Spirit are three in one. The good thing is, as in life, we start out as children. He helps us grow and learn how to live for Him here on earth. It takes time. Cam and I are still growing and learning by reading our Bible, praying, and talking with other believers. That's another beautiful thing, it all, well, happens. When you are seeking Him and learning His ways, you simply know. Oh, my goodness, I sure have said a lot in the last few minutes."

"But why did He allow me to be in an accident if He loves me so much? Wouldn't He have protected me?" I ask.

"I have to put that into that mystery category again of not having all the answers this side of Heaven. It says in the Bible that the rain falls on everyone, so accepting Him or His love for us is not like a magic genie or a fairy tale where we never experience what life offers anymore. I mean, bald men don't suddenly grow hair! We don't suddenly have perfect figures. We have free choice, we live in a fallen world, and we always are fighting our enemy the devil who the Bible says prowls around like a roaring lion, looking to kill and destroy. So, does He protect us from things? Yes, often, but some things are allowed. We still go through the problems of life, some of which we cause, some we don't. We do have the promise that whatever happens to us as believers, He will work it for good when we are living for His purposes. That means He will work it for good, even if in itself it isn't good. This life can be wonderful, but it's not perfect, and it's not Heaven," she says.

"That's for sure!" I say.

"There are so many things we don't know, or we view it through our limited lens, like we wouldn't have done it that way. But we aren't God. We don't see 'the rest of our story' yet, and we may never have all the answers for everything on this side of Heaven. There are tough questions, like why those we love die well before old age. But everyone, absolutely everyone is given the chance of eternal life with the Father, Son, and Holy Spirit in Heaven where we will live much longer than we ever will live on earth. That's our forever home."

"And all of this is in the Bible?" I ask.

"Yes … and it's the living word of God, meaning, it can speak to each of us in different ways at different times at our point of need. That's why it's so important to start reading the Bible and not just learn a few stories. I spent my growing up years tuning out what I was hearing about Jesus. It was just religion to me and something my parents made me do," she says.

"I have to say, I don't understand much of this, but I understand enough to know that I need to read the book of John. I want to read it in the light of all the information you gave me."

"I think that's a great idea, and I have a little list of more verses that you will find helpful. There is a guide in the front of each Bible that tells you the name of the book and what page it starts at. Then you just look up the chapter and verse. You said the Bible you got is a modern version, right?" she asks.

"Yes, I think it is. I remember my uncle saying that."

"That's helpful. I grew up reading the King James with the 'thee's and thou's' and when Sister Mary-Margaret encouraged me to read a modern language Bible, that made all the difference for me. Speaking of Sister Mary-Margaret, she will be here soon, and I cannot wait for you to meet her! Do you want me to pray with you right now about what you've learned?"

"I think I want to wait and read these verses. I don't want to do it in the heat of the moment. I need to understand," I say, hoping I'm not offending her.

"I get it. I was the same way. I think if you pray, which is talking to God like you're talking to me right now, read the Bible, and look at the verses on the list or anything else you find to read, you will find your answers. Be aware that you may feel a tug on your heart from the Holy Spirit. No one becomes a believer because the person who is telling them the story of salvation is an eloquent speaker or a great persuader. It happens because the Holy Spirit is calling them," she says.

"Thank you for this list. I'll tuck it in my pocket here, and this time, I promise, I will look at John and what you have given me. It feels different this time. Listening for the Holy Spirit sounds a little scary to me, but I can see on your face that you don't see it that way. I will be open to whatever happens because I do believe you. And Sister Mary-Margaret sounds amazing, I hope I get some free time to meet her," I say.

"I've told you about the hard road it can be to follow Jesus, but the goodness and love of God surpasses everything we might go through here on earth. It's like you being able to play all those instruments. You didn't just wish you could, you spent hours and years learning how to be a good musician. It was hard, but most good things are. And now, look at your reward! You can play anything; music gives you immense pleasure, and you're playing and singing brings joy to others. And now, you might play with J.D.! It's the outcome of doing it the right way to get to where you are. That's what it's like to walk the Christian life. It's not easy, but the outcome beats anything else. I hope you understand that, too. You have a loving God, His Son Jesus, and the Holy Spirit who will never leave you, will always guide you, and eventually you spend eternity with them in Heaven! Sometimes I have to sit down and tell myself, it's real!

This is real. It's all true! Piper says. "And another fantastic, unexplainable thing …? Jesus relates personally to us as individuals. You'll see as you read the Bible. Every interaction He had with each person was unique to them, and that's how He relates to each of us, too."

The buzzer rings, and we both jump a mile!

"Oh my gosh, we were both so 'not here' for a moment, that scared me. That's a buzzer signal from Freddy to come down. He's either super busy or he's having a mini emergency. That's what that special buzzer means. I hate to bolt downstairs, but he probably really needs me," Piper says jumping up.

"Don't give it a second thought. Thank you for taking the time you did with me. Thank you, Piper, for caring!"

"I do care, Alice. Here I go, take your time, and come down when you're ready," she says with a nervous look of needing to get downstairs quickly.

What a conversation! I really want to read my Bible! How could I be almost thirty years old and never know any of this? Sounds like something is going on downstairs, maybe they need my help. I hate to go down with too many people there and draw attention to my face, but I have to go sometime. Here goes. Hmm, people seem to be huddled around a guy. I can't tell who he is with his back to me. It sounds like he's saying something about he would be happy to … maybe he's a local artist? It doesn't look like there's an emergency at least. Wait, Piper looks frozen to the counter, and she's mouthing something to me. What? She's pointing to the huddle and mouthing the words; That's J.D. Grayling!

CHAPTER THIRTEEN

Oh my gosh, this is it! I have to introduce myself. I don't want him to meet me later and wonder why I didn't say something. What do I look like? My conversation with Piper probably made my makeup run. Can I sneak in a bathroom before I meet him, or will that look weird if I walk back upstairs? What will Piper think? My hair is a mess from the wind on the walk here, and …

"Alice, come on down here and meet someone!" Piper says with a big smile.

Drat, too late to turn around and fix myself. He will probably only see the patch anyway.

"J.D., thanks so much for shopping with us today, but I want you to meet someone who is a part of your crew. This is my friend, Alice Merveille," Piper says.

Watching J.D. turn around to face me feels like one of those pivotal moments in a movie where everything goes into slow motion. If it's possible for your heart to leap out of your chest from pounding so hard, it's going to happen right now!

"Hey Alice. Well, this is a coincidence! I've heard so many good things about your talents. I know you're going to be a great asset to us this summer," J.D. says, shaking my hand.

"Hi, J.D. Thank you. I'm excited to be here and a little speechless. I'm a huge fan of your music, so excuse me if I sound a little crazy right now," I say.

That was dumb. I can't think of something clever to say. I hope he didn't feel how sweaty my palm is.

"I appreciate that, Alice. It's always nice to hear someone likes my music. That's the kind of encouragement that keeps me going," J.D. says. "I mean it sincerely; I understand you are quite a musician. I can't wait to jam together."

"I'd love that. All the instruments are here, and everything looks to be in order," I say.

"Oh, good. That's always half the battle, making sure the instruments are up to snuff. Listen, folks, this has been fun, but if you have my art supplies wrapped up there, I probably should get going. If I don't show up where I'm supposed to be, my manager will cause a ruckus, and we can't have that. I just slipped in here to grab some supplies, so I can do a few projects if I get a chance. I didn't mean to disrupt what you have going on here. Thanks for putting this together for me, Freddy," J.D. says, scooping up his bag of art supplies. "And Piper, you have a cool store here. I'm sure I'll be back for more things. I hope you can all make a show while we're performing on the island, and Alice, I'll see you soon. Bye everyone."

As he heads out the door, we all seem to be in shock. I'm staring at Piper. She's staring at me, and our mouths are hanging open.

"You get to work with him this summer?" a lady in a blue hat asks. "Lucky you, I'd give my right arm to hang out with J.D.!"

"Oh my gosh, he's even more handsome in person than he is on his album covers and that voice! It's like liquid velvet. I'm going to go to his show for sure. And we got his autograph; do you believe it?" another lady says to the blue hat lady as they scurry out the door together.

"Well, that was the biggest celebrity I ever waited on before, and he liked the art supplies I put together for him. That was really cool!" Freddy says.

"I'm pretty star-struck too. I did work with Christopher Reeve and Jane Seymour, at a distance of course, but meeting such a big music star? You are going to have quite a few weeks ahead of you Alice!" Piper says squealing with delight.

"He's such a gentleman, no cracks about my face, and yes, he is even better looking in person than he looks on his album covers," I say. "But now, I'm more nervous. He just became a real person, not a poster image on my closet door. I hope I can live up to what he thinks I'm capable of when it comes to playing music. I mean, how can I play an instrument when my palms are pouring sweat and my knees are shaking?" I ask.

"You will do fantastic. All new things are hard. You'll get over those jitters, you'll see. Your years of training will come to your rescue, and you'll make his performances even better with what you are doing in the background. We believe in you, Alice. It's your time to shine!" Piper says. "Well, back to reality for us. Hey, Freddy, would you mind running upstairs and making sure that order is ready to go out in the mail tomorrow? That would be a great help."

"Sure thing, Pip," he says, winking at me. "I'll get right on it. Great to see you, Miss Alice. Don't forget your bag of art supplies, laying right there. I think you'll like what I picked out," he adds, pointing at the bag next to the register.

"Oh my gosh, thank you for doing that. Let me pay you for those," I say.

"No way. Those are on the house, to get you started in your art. Our treat," Piper says.

"You enjoy and let me know if you need something else," Freddy says, heading up the stairs. "Toodle ooo, Miss Alice, have a blessed day!"

"Thanks Freddy. I really appreciate it," I say.

"Well, Alice, I think this day will go down as — do you keep a journal by the way? If you don't, you should start one. I think you're going to have a lot to write about. Meeting J.D. was awesome, but I hope you get a chance to think about our conversation. I'm so happy we had that time together, so I could tell you more about my heart's passion. I do wish I knew what you were thinking," Piper says.

"Honestly? Any thought I had about anything fell out when J.D. was standing there! But seriously, I will think about what you said. I should start a journal; that's good advice. I'm feeling about a million different things right now, and they all add up to be quite overwhelming. But I see you're talking to me out of concern. I don't know where I am with everything, and I don't want to take what you shared with me lightly. I'm kind of a processing person. I need some alone time to think about what you said. And I am going to read the Bible. I mean, I have that one anyway — kind of a coincidence, I guess."

"Ah, that word — coincidence. J.D. said it, too. One thing Sister Mary-Margaret taught me, oh, listen to me, she taught me so many things, but this one really hit me. There are no coincidences. There are God's plans, always there waiting. The difference comes when we choose to join Him in what He's doing, or we don't. It all comes down to that. So, it's not a coincidence you got that Bible and then met me. It was planned," Piper says.

"Hmm. And if I follow your thinking, it's not a coincidence I got to meet J.D. when everyone in the band wasn't around. I've never looked at anything that way, that there aren't coincidences. I've been running under the radar for so many years. I've always been the girl with the disfigured face and the eye patch, well, ever since I became an adult at eighteen and was in the accident," I say.

"I hope you don't think I'm nosy, but what happened?" Piper asks.

"Of course, you wonder. I would too if I saw someone who

looks like me. The accident happened when my mother was driving. She had a drinking problem. I guess I didn't realize it so much growing up, but as I got a little older, I saw it for what it was. She hit a tree, and we both got knocked out. She woke up first and got out of her side and came around to help me, but a fire broke out first. The paramedics got there a little while later, and she had pulled me out, but not before I was burned. I'm happy to be alive, but that day did change everything about me and my future. Then it all came about the girl with the ugly face," I say turning away.

"Oh, Alice, I'm so sorry you have had to live through that. How hard for you, not to mention painful, I'm sure. You are filled with courage to keep going and take on this new adventure," she says.

"Ha, well. It wasn't courage to take this job. I didn't have a choice. It was my uncle's chance to rent out his higher end instruments, sell them as used by major artists after this summer, and sell his music shop in Cheboygan. He basically kicked me out and said I owed him this for all the medical bills from my accident and my mother's cancer. I made him promise we were square if I did this. So, you see, my coming here wasn't courage. It was being painted into a corner with nowhere else to go," I say.

"I still think you are courageous for all you've been through."

"Well thank you. Now a musician I've admired forever actually knows my name and it sounds like, so does the Creator of the world. Let's just say, I'm beyond speechless. But, Piper, I will tell you this. I'm really happy *you* know my name. You are the type of friend I've been hoping for all my life. So, thank you for everything today," I say.

"We talked about some pretty important things, but there is something else you should know. He's a magnificent God with good gifts for His children. And living a life for Him is the most exciting life you could ever choose. It's hard to explain to someone, but when you experience it for yourself, you'll understand. Can I give you a hug?" Piper asks.

With my nod she puts her arms around me and hugs me tightly. Little does she know; I've not been hugged by another human being since my mom passed almost four years ago. The tears start to flow. What world have I walked into?

CHAPTER FOURTEEN

Oh, yes, Mr. Sun. I see you peeking through my window. Hello. I guess I will open my eyes wider and not wait for the alarm clock to ring. At least I slept a little. Yesterday. Yesterday was a doozy. It was a good idea to take it down a notch and have dinner in my room. Then that nice hot shower — exactly what I needed to help me sleep. Let's see, if I had to pick a number from one to ten of where my nerves were when I got back to my room, I'd easily say ten! I don't remember the walk back or opening my door. One good thing, the instruments are all set and ready to go. That's a major thing done on my checklist. True, the note under my door set me on edge again. It ran through my mind every time I woke up a little.

Miss Merveille,

The whole group will meet tomorrow morning after breakfast at 10 a.m. sharp.

See you then,

M. Cheshire

Yes, now that I think about it, I was having dreams about instruments breaking and Montague yelling at me in front of everyone. I don't care about him, but I do want to live up to J.D.'s expectations. It's a good thing I got to meet J.D. before

Montague Cheshire gave his opinion of me, at least I hope that's what happened. Enough conjecture. *Get up Alice and face the music.* I seem to be doing that a lot lately.

I'll keep it casual with jeans and my favorite blouse. I do love it — the flowing navy-blue gauze; with the little forget-me-nots crocheted around the yoke. I couldn't believe I found it on the rack at the thrift store. If I could have more blouses like this, that would be perfect. I need every good feeling I can get.

What will happen if I say a prayer right now as I head down the stairs toward the meeting? I didn't read the Bible yet, so is it okay to say a prayer? Hmm. I'm not going to let people think I'm crazy. I'll just think it in my head. Can't hurt. Dear God, help me today. I'm scared and nervous. Help me. Amen. Okay, no lightning bolts or anything. I guess I pray now. I've got to get to that Bible reading sooner rather than later. After today, I should be able to concentrate on something other than this job for a few minutes.

Yes, all these people walking in seem like band people. I'll keep smiling, nodding, and head for the chairs set up where everyone else seems to be going. Am I supposed to introduce myself? That seems too forward. This seat looks good. I feel safer here in the back row. There goes Montague to the little podium in the front of the chairs. Vivian is sitting next to J.D. in the front row. They are both so gorgeous — like a movie star couple.

"Welcome, everyone, on behalf of J.D. and myself. And so, we begin our summer gig on this incredible island. If you haven't had a chance to look around yet, you're in for a beautiful surprise. Most of us know each other, but we have a couple new people so let's make a few introductions. I think it's easiest if when I say your name, you each come up here and tell us a little about yourself," Montague says. "As in any band, no one ever goes by a person's real name. So, you new people, enjoy this rare moment. I'll go first, although I think I've met everyone in the group. I'm Montague Cheshire, and

I've been J.D.'s manager for too many years to count now, right J.D.?"

"Way too many years, Monty!" J.D. says with a laugh.

"You know I'm the best thing that ever happened to you," Montague says with a look of intense pride. "And for any new people, only J.D. calls me, uh, Monty. Only he does."

Lots of sideway glances are happening, but no one says a peep. We all know he's not kidding. Yes, there's the guy I've met, not a smidge of humility, and an expert at creating awkward moments.

"Up next, a rhythm guitar king, Simon 'Doogey' Taylor. Doogey?" Montague says.

A tall, lanky guy with hair down to the middle of his back heads to the podium with a noticeable limp.

"Hey cats, glad to be on this tour with J.D. One of my favorite things in the world is to be playing with him and watching the crowds light up. Glad to be here on this amazing island. I mean, no cars! How far out is that. I'm looking forward to a fun time and to get to know the new people. I hail from Tennessee, so I'm also looking forward to a cooler summer here on these beautiful shores," Doogey says and turns to limp back to his seat.

"Thanks, Doogey. Uh, don't mind the limp. Doogey jumped off one too many stages, but he's on the mend. Let's see, how about Joey 'Jammer' Holloway next," Montague says.

Running up to the podium, Jammer reminds me of a rabbit, ready to hop down a trail, brimming with energy. And yes, he has buck teeth in the front.

"Stoked to be here. Looking forward to the new jams, the new digs, the new people, and hanging with you all. Gonna be an awesome summer. I'm from Colorado, and man, there are no mountains around here. But it's alright. I'm into these Straits and that bridge. I dig it!" he says.

"Thanks, Jammer. Up now, Barry 'Bongo' Crispin," Montague says calling up one of the tallest guys I've ever seen.

He has to be almost seven feet tall, at least he looks that way to me.

"Cool, cool, cool, Montague. Keeping it cool as always, loving the chance to play the skins on this magical place. Any time we can hang with J.D. is always a trip, and I'm thrilled to be along for this ride, man. Chillin '," Bongo says. He's straight out of a 1960s beatnik movie complete with the goatee and beret. He seems fun.

"New to us and this tour, welcome, Andy 'Strings' Archer," Montague says, pointing to another tall but very skinny dude. I think you have to be skinny to be in a band.

"Thanks, Montague. I'm fresh off a tour with James Jenquin," Andy says.

"Props man — great artist, stellar band," Bongo yells from his seat.

"Thanks Bongo. They are amazing, but I am equally in awe of J.D. and you guys. So, getting to play with you is a dream come true. You may notice I don't speak like a Yank, ha! I'm from Liverpool but do love playing here in the States whenever I can. Never heard of this place before, but it is one of the most beautiful places I've seen. I've just started to see all it has to offer. Glad to be a part of the group, and you know I will bring it on my bass," Strings says.

"So, that's The Madhatter's ensemble for this gig. Of course, we are most fortunate to have here this summer J.D.'s special lady, Vivian. Vivian, you want to introduce yourself?" Montague says with a hand swoosh as if he's greeting royalty.

"Oh, thanks for including me, Montague. With the hotel in my family, I know this island inside and out. I'd be happy to be a tour guide for any of you or give guidance on things to see and do in your free time. My job is to make sure you are all pampered and treated well so you have the best time of your life. Please, anything I can do, just let me know," Vivian says with a wink and a curtsey.

The group gives her a big round of applause at hearing she wants to pamper us. Well, them, I guess. She really is a beauty.

"Let's see, yes. Here's a new person — Miranda Colter. She is going to be our liaison for anything you need, including keeping us filled up with coffee and snacks. Miranda?" Montague says gesturing her forward. She seems like the matronly aunt you always wish you had.

"Hi, guys and gals. I'm Miranda, and I've been doing this for years with different bands. Was I at Woodstock? Yes, I was! You know a band has made it when they bring me on their tour," she says with a big laugh. Everyone is laughing back at this entertaining lady. "Anything you like, don't like, or need, I'm your gal. I mean if I have to pick out a certain color of M&Ms to keep any of you happy, I'll do it! Any day-to-day items you're lacking, or even if you're not sure who to ask about those type of things, I'm the one. I used to come to the island for vacation as a kid, so I have a history here. Afterall, who do you think it was that introduced Vivian to J.D.? The favor is being returned by bringing me on this gig so I can see my family afterward, and yes, I am pretty useful," she says with a wink toward J.D. as she heads back to her seat. I thought Vivian said they met when she was modeling. This makes a little more sense. He didn't seek out Vivian. She had an introduction. Vivian must have set this catering gig up for her. As they say, it's who you know that gets you ahead.

"Yes, please make sure I only get red M&Ms in my dressing room, Miranda," Montague says with a chuckle, but I highly doubt he is kidding. Thank goodness the Grand Hotel is too small for dressing rooms. The last thing he needs is something more to build his ego. I hate this feeling, like amped up nerves on steroids all because he has to be calling on my very soon.

"Everyone, please say hello to Sally Wagner. Sally is in charge of ticketing among many other things. Any comp tickets you want to request for guests and payroll — she's your contact. So, you might want to be extra nice to her. The label was gracious enough to lend her to us for a few weeks to help with our details but also to work on some label things with J.D. She will also be spending time getting some relaxation with friends here on the island, so you won't see her every day. Feel free to leave a message for her, and she'll get back to you. She's another Michigan girl, and we're glad this all worked out that she could jump in here and still keep up with all her responsibilities at the label. Welcome, Sally."

"Hey, everyone! Yes, this is my old stomping grounds, Michigan that is, but getting to stay here is a dream come true, and of course, working with J.D., more of a dream come true. As Montague said, any comp tickets, payroll, any of that kind of stuff, I'm your person. Nice to meet all of you. Stop by this podium before you leave and pick up my business card. It has my contact information. You can leave a message with the concierge as well; I'll check for my messages as often as I can. The label keeps me hopping. It can be a pressure-packed world, so I am going to enjoy a little fresh island as much as I can," Sally says walking back to her seat.

I think I'm the only one left to talk. Here goes nothing.

"Well, except for our fearless leader, that about does it, I think," Montague says, turning to J.D.

"J.D., let's hear from you now!"

The group starts to clap, and I'm not sure if I'm insulted or relieved, but it's clear he really doesn't feel like I'm part of this group. All eyes follow J.D. up to the podium as he looks at all of us.

"I'm stoked for the upcoming concerts, because I think it's going to be one of the best tours we've ever had. But, first, Monty, you left out probably the most important person in our group, and I want to bring her forward right now. Hey gang, please welcome Alice Merveille!" J.D. says gesturing me up to the podium.

I can't believe my legs are working because I feel numb, but somehow, here I am standing next to him at the podium.

"I think Monty didn't have enough coffee or something this morning, because we all know if we don't have an amazing tech, everything can go south really fast," J.D. says giving a dirty look to Montague who seems to be preoccupied with looking in his folder.

"Thanks, J.D. I'm happy to be here. I'm Alice Merveille, but I guess you said that. All the instruments are looking great so far and anything you need in special tuning or adjustment, let me know. If you prefer different strings, pedals, even a favorite pick color, I can make it happen. I look forward to a great summer. I'm from about thirty minutes away in a small town called Cheboygan. Those of us who live close don't get the chance to stay on the island, so this is a real thrill for me, too. I'm happy to answer any questions," I say smiling at J.D. He puts his arm around my shoulder and gives me a squeeze. Turning to me he takes both of my hands and says, "We are really glad you are here with us this summer, really glad."

Montague jumps up and pushes his way between the two of us.

"Well, sorry there missy, didn't mean to skip you. No hard feelings, right dearie? Okay, everyone, our first rehearsal starts after lunch, so let's regroup at 1:30 p.m. back on stage. I have a table reserved for us, so meet for lunch at noon at the entrance to the dining hall," Montague says.

"Don't count on me for any meals, Montague," Sally says. "I've got friend stuff lined up, and if I get a chance to join in, I'll let you know."

"Well, that works out perfectly because our reservation is for eight," Montague says with that big grin he does.

"I think you lost your ability to count, Monty," J.D. says. "Vivian, Doogey, Jammer, Strings, Bongo, Miranda, Alice, and you make nine."

"Oh, Alice, I guess I wasn't thinking she would be part of the group for meals …," Montague says giving me another dirty look.

"You know what, pal? I think the reservation for eight works just fine. You sit this one out; how about that? Then next time, you will be better at counting when we all eat together. That works, right?" J.D. says with his voice growing more intense.

"Uh, sure, J.D. I have a lot to do anyway, whatever you think," Montague says, turning and leaving the room quickly.

I can't believe what just happened. I should pray more often!

CHAPTER FIFTEEN

That was a memorable lunch, especially without Montague. But it will probably come back to bite me. He'll blame the lunch head count fiasco — which he caused — on me. And what stories from the guys in the band! Hilarious! They should all write a book about their lives in a band on the road. When J.D. gestured for me to sit next to him, I didn't care what Vivian was thinking. I just wanted to sit there and soak it all up. His questions were so attentive and sweet, asking me about my favorite things to play. I hope I didn't talk too much. I liked listening to what everyone else had to say.

The food! That has to be the longest food bar any of us have ever seen with anything anyone could want. Fish, beef, chicken, and every color of vegetable, a wide variety of salads, various hors d'oeuvres, appetizers, and mouth-watering desserts in abundance. I'm not sure how we will all be able to stay awake for practice after such a feast, but it was fun to feel like a part of the group.

Splitting up with a half hour before we meet, it feels good to have a moment to be in the music room before everyone arrives. I know things are ready, but after what happened to my guitar, I can't be too sure. Oh good, the room is still locked. That must have been an accident about my guitar. I'm glad I didn't call the police. The guys should be here any minute and can grab whatever instrument they want to start out with. I hope J.D. notices I've set up his mic stand with fifteen picks lined up so he can grab one and throw it out in the crowd after a big song. I remember reading in a magazine that his fans love that in his concerts.

"Yoo hoo, Alice. It's Miranda."

"Hi, Miranda. Are you feeling as full as I am?" I ask.

"I know, and here I am about to wheel in a snack cart! It's just some fruit, candy, and crackers, iced tea, juice, and coffee. What's your drink of choice? Are you a tea drinker?"

"Oh, I'll probably stick with water. Don't worry about me. I have a weird allergy to tea, and with what I ate at lunch, I don't need to eat anything for a long time. I don't know how people do breakfast, lunch, and dinner here ... with such amazing food. A person could put on a few pounds, that's for sure,"

"I agree. I guess if you want to eat here, you have to get out on the island and hike around, or yes, you'll blow up like a balloon!" she says. "So, what do you think of J.D.? Isn't he something else? Do you have a crush like the rest of us?"

I hope she's kidding.

"Yes," I say with a laugh, "I have the same crush the entire world has — in love with his music," I say.

"Oh, are you sure it's not something more? Wouldn't he make a dreamy boyfriend?" she asks.

"Well, he has a beautiful girlfriend, and I'm sure they are very happy."

This questioning is strange. I need to change the subject.

"Oh, don't mind me. I'm just feeling my age and longing for the days of my youth when I was still in the running with all these rock stars. I've met so many. I used to be in the mix, but I've crossed some kind of line where I look more like their old aunt. It's hard to accept," she says wistfully.

"You are a beautiful lady, and I'm sure you have lots of

remarkable stories. And I've noticed some very handsome men of all ages here on the island. Maybe you will meet someone this summer," I say.

I hope that's not too forward, but obviously this lady needs a pep talk. Not my area of expertise, but at least I can offer an encouraging word.

"Yes, I've seen a few. I guess I have to change my thinking from 'rock star' to gentlemen of a certain age. I wouldn't mind meeting a really rich guy this summer and living a life I would like to become accustomed to," she says.

"Well, maybe that will happen," I say.

"Enjoy your youth while you still have it. Unfortunately, it fades, and so will you. It happens to everyone," she says.

Thanks, Miranda. Maybe I need a pep talk right about now!

"Oh, with my face, I don't have any expectations of the beauty of youth. That's long gone for me," I say.

"Yeah, but I saw how you looked at J.D. at lunch. You have a thing for him I think," she says.

"No, what you're seeing is admiration for a fellow musician. That's all. I'm starstruck like any fan that meets someone they have enjoyed," I say.

"Well, just making sure. I don't want to see you get your heart broken. I've seen it over and over again with theses stars. Young girls get the wrong idea," she says.

I guess she has been around and does know the score far more than I do. She probably has good advice.

"Ladies, how's it going?" Vivian asks, pushing the door open. "All set for a great practice?"

"I've got the snacks all set up, so when they need a break, they will have what they need," Miranda says. "I know these guys get hungry fast. Beats me how they all stay so skinny!"

"Oh, you're the best. I know you always get J.D.'s favorites. How about you leave these musicians to their thing Miranda, and I'll take you on a tour of downtown," Vivian says.

"Shopping! Yes, I'm up for that! I want to get something for my sister. She's been so sick," Miranda says.

"Don't miss The Creative Lilac. It's a great store filled with all kinds of art supplies and art for sale," I say. Might as well get in a plug for Piper's place.

"Oh, we're more of a clothes, shoes, hats, and purses kind of gals, aren't we Miranda? Sure, we'll find a trinket for your sister," Vivian says.

"As long as it's shopping, I love it," Miranda says as she interlocks her arm with Vivian, and they both give a wave as they leave. Thank goodness! It can be me and the band without them butting in every couple of minutes. They are okay, but I don't see us becoming best friends. I don't feel anything about them like I do about Piper and Cam. This isn't my best thought, but the word "shallow" comes to mind.

The guys should be getting here any minute. I'm ready. Let's do some music already! One more quick tuning of J.D.'s twelve string. I want it to be perfect.

Running my finger along the frets and doing some picking leads me right into his hit, "Raincheck." I know the best test is to mess around with a guitar riff, adding a little flare. With my fingers flying through the chords, I realize how much I've missed playing music since I arrived. This is soothing and invigorating to me all at the same time, just how it feels when I'm soaking in the island air and moonlight. Music is meant for this island, and this island for music.

"Whoa, whoa, are you kidding me? Keep that up, and you're going to put me out of a job!" Doogey says standing next to me. I was so far gone I didn't hear him come in.

"You have that riff nailed. Do you know how long it took me to learn that? You make it look easy, and believe me, I know it's not!"

"What's not easy?" asks J.D., also suddenly in the room.

"Mind blown. You know that crazy riff in 'Raincheck' that

I've always cursed you for writing? The one we throw in, in live shows?" Doogey asks.

"Yes, I'm familiar with it," J.D. says, laughing.

"Well, if you heard it on your way in, that wasn't me. That was Alice. And she added things I would never attempt, and made it look easy," Doogey says.

"Really? Let's hear it, Alice," J.D. says.

"Nah, I'm sure you guys want to get going," I say.

And here comes Jammer, Strings, and Bongo — all looking at me. Yikes! How did I get myself into this situation?

"Alice! Alice! Alice!" they all chant. Should I smile or run out as fast as I can?

"Come on, Alice. Show us. We are rooting for you, and we all love a sharp musician," J.D. says with a wink.

"Okay, but my palms are sweating, so I may goof up," I say.

I take a deep breath, start the song, and dive in. They all start singing along, and I find a third harmony no one is doing and join in. As we get closer to the riff, they all drop out and focus on me. Oh, brother — rather Oh, Lord — make this good!

In what feels like another out-of-body experience, my fingers fly, and I hit every single note with a few little improvisations thrown in. I hit the last strum, and I'm afraid to look up. I think I did okay, but these guys are all professionals. There's a moment of dead silence when my heart stops, and they all burst into applause and are shouting my name!

"Alice, Alice, Alice!"

"Uh, guys, we are in the presence of a maestro!" J.D. says, and they all clap again.

Oh, these guys! This is as close as I've ever felt to finally feeling validated as a musician. It's so wonderful.

"What are you doing as a tech, mate, and not performing? And what about your voice? It rocks!" Strings says.

"Absolutely amazing," Bongo says. "I knew they said we had

a talented tech working with us this summer, but wow, just wow."

"And you play all the instruments?" Jammer asks.

"Guys, you are embarrassing me. I'm new at this. I've been at a little music store teaching myself for most of my life, so believe me, I have no idea what I'm doing," I say, sure that my face is fifty shades of red. "Yes, I can play all the instruments."

"Can you play mandolin, fiddle, and cello?" J.D. asks.

"Yes," I say.

They all set into whooping and hollering again.

"You see, I had no life, so I played music all the time …" I say.

"Well, that's awesome news for us, because you have a new life beginning right now. We still need you to tech of course, but if you're willing, we will also have you doing some performing with us too," J.D. says with a smile. "What do you think guys? Want to perform with Alice?"

Choruses of yes, can't wait, and super cool arise, and I think I'm going to faint from pure joy.

"Not so fast, J.D."

Oh great. Montague Cheshire, the wet blanket has entered the room and brought a cloud of doom along with him. I should have known this was too good to be true.

CHAPTER SIXTEEN

"Monty, we have a virtuoso here, and we are going to make her part of this summer," J.D. says, turning to Montague with his arms crossed.

"J.D., there are musician union rules, tech rules, and things out of our control. We can't simply ignore contracts …," Montague says with his snakey smile.

Oh please, J.D., please catch onto this fake man and don't be fooled by him any longer.

"Then do your job. Get new contracts, adjust the pay scale, work with the union, but get it done," J.D. says, turning and grabbing his twelve string and heading for the stage. "Come on guys, grab your stuff, and let's get going. Alice, if you want to finish up in here, join us on stage in a couple of minutes, and we will go over each of our tech needs, and talk about how we can fit you in on various numbers. Can't wait, excellent job!"

Turning to me with a smile, I see it morph into a frown as he faces Montague.

"No problem, J.D. I'm sure I can work something out," Montague says. The only time I see the weasel fold is when he speaks to J.D.

As the guys are leaving my heart sinks. It's going to be me

and Montague in this room alone for a moment. *Think positive, Alice. Maybe we can finally get this cleared up and find out what his problem is.*

"Well, I guess they need me on stage," I say, heading toward the door.

"You really think you're something, don't you?", Montague asks. Okay, so much for positive thinking.

"Listen, Montague, I don't know why you are so down on me, but I'm only here to do a good job. I have no desire to threaten you or get in your way, yet you seem to be going out of your way to make my life difficult. I didn't do anything to deserve all this treatment from you," I say.

"Oh, you think J.D. likes you, huh? He is known for gathering broken and stray things. That's the attraction. If you didn't have that patch and face, he wouldn't be giving you the time of day. So now you are this great musician too? Well, you aren't the first. I've seen your type. You play it all innocent, thinking you're going to be his new love, and that you're going to run the show. Well, get it straight. I run this show!"

He's spitting, and his face is contorting and growing redder by the minute. He's keeping it to a loudly whispered hiss, so the others can't hear him.

"As I said, I'm only here to do a job and keep the instruments sounding great or anything else J.D. requests in the line of music. Whatever you think of my motives, you are way off. I'm just a nobody who happens to be a good musician. That's it. No agenda. No desire to run anything. So, don't lump me in with any past escapades," I say.

"Are you accusing me of something? See, that's what you do, with words like escapades. That's accusatory. Another reason I don't trust you and can't wait for you to be done with this tour. This will be the end of your relationship with this band, if you even make it that long. I haven't been J.D.'s manager all these years without knowing how he ticks and what decisions he makes in the end. You can be sure of that, missy."

As he turns to leave, J.D. pops his head in. "Everything okay in here? You getting it all settled with Alice, Monty?"

"Oh yes, right as rain, my friend. We are *very* clear. As always, I'll make sure everything turns out just as it should, you know that about me. Sorry about that lunch reservation mix-up before Alice, totally not like me to miss out on someone as important as you. That won't happen again. Off now to get those contracts fixed, and don't you worry, Alice, you will get yours — a salary bump I mean because of the extra playing and things you'll be doing. I'm sure it will be satisfactory. I'll work it out with the various 'powers-that-be.' I know how to deal with all kinds," Montague says with his usual chameleon switch when J.D. is around.

"Great, love to hear that, Monty. You ready, Alice? The guys are itching to throw in some cello and mandolin where we haven't been able to before. Man, you are a godsend!"

Passing Montague and getting one more look of hate, I don't feel like a godsend, but I sure hope God sends help!

CHAPTER SEVENTEEN

What a practice! The guys and I mesh perfectly. Knowing all the songs made it so easy to jump right in. Mandolin, cello — I think I added some flare they haven't always had outside the studio. It seemed to get everyone even more excited to perform. They were all so complimentary, and every time J.D. said something nice, my heart started to pound faster. It's like a dream come true, more than I ever imagined was possible. Turning the key in my door after this unbelievable day, I feel like I'm floating. Once I got past Montague, it was wonderful. Then this note from Piper under my door, probably put there by Cam, asking if I can pop in soon because Sister Mary-Margaret will be there. Okay, I know my assignment for the evening; read those Bible verses. I'm not gonna lie to a nun if she asks if I looked up some verses. Come on!

Alright, I'll settle in at this cozy desk in my room and do this. I'd rather daydream about this day, but a promise, is a promise.

First one, John 3:16 and 17.

For God so loved the world that he gave his one and only Son, that whoever believes in him shall not perish but have eternal life. For God did not send his Son into the world to condemn the world, but to save the world through him.

This is the one Piper said where I could put my name, I get it. *For God so loved Alice.* Wow, that brings it home. God, it says here You love me so much You gave Your Son to die in my place, to save me. That's amazing. Next one.

Romans 10:9-10.

If you declare with your mouth, "Jesus is Lord," and believe in your heart that God raised him from the dead, you will be saved. For it is with your heart that you believe and are justified, and it is with your mouth that you profess your faith and are saved.

That's along the same lines. Declare with your mouth and believe in your heart, so it sounds like if you do it, you're not supposed to keep it to yourself or hide it away.

Now, 1 Peter 1:3.

Praise be to the God and Father of our Lord Jesus Christ! In his great mercy he has given us new birth into a living hope through the resurrection of Jesus Christ from the dead.

I become new, with new hope because of what Jesus did? New me, new hope, that's all good. There's a pattern here! I wish it could also mean "new face."

Now, Ephesians 2:8. These Bible chapter titles are quite different, that's for sure.

For it is by grace you have been saved, through faith — and this is not from yourselves, it is the gift of God.

So, it's what God did. This makes it clear that being a good person isn't what God is looking for. I mean, I'm sure He wants people to act right, but that's now how we are saved. It's a gift from Him that saves us — why He sent Jesus to die on the cross and come back to life. And we all have the choice to take the gift or refuse it. Have I been refusing this gift without even knowing it? That's the question I keep coming back to. I just didn't know this stuff, but now that I do, what am I going to do? Hmm. So, yes, I want this. Who wouldn't? Why would anyone say "no?" I don't get it. Unless, they don't like the part Piper talked about, what was it she said, changing up your life or … No, it was making Jesus Lord of our life. That's what she said and doing things the way He would instead of what I think. I wouldn't mind the direction; I don't feel great about making my own decisions about which way to go. I feel lost, and this feels like an answer. But do I have to not be me anymore, not play music? Piper said to take it one step at a time, to accept the gift first, and He will work out the rest like a loving father.

Loving father? What's that like? That girl in my class seemed to really like her dad. Am I overthinking this? Yeah, that's me. These verses make it clear that God loves me, that He sent Jesus to die for me personally, and He wants me to decide about accepting the gift He put out there. But why didn't he stop the accident that stole a normal life from me? I'm a little confused.

I need sleep. P.J.'s on, under the covers, lights out, and all I can see is the look on J.D.'s face when I played a riff he didn't expect, but welcomed. My mind is darting all over the place. Will I dream about Heaven, or J.D. tonight? But what if God does ask me to give up music and to stop playing with J.D.? Could He do that? Would He do that? And why *did* I have to lose my face and my mother? Sister Mary-Margaret, what will you have to say about that?!

CHAPTER EIGHTEEN

Ringing. Ringing. Bells ringing. Oh my gosh, wake up, Alice! My phone. I don't think it ever rang in my room, let alone while I'm still sleeping. Probably Piper wondering if I can make it today.

"Hello?"

"Alice! Wake up sleepy head. You sound like you're still sleeping!"

Oh my gosh, it's J.D.!

"Hi, J.D.! What time is it? Let's see — Oh, six a.m. What are you doing up so early? Is everything okay?"

"Yeah, this is early, guess I didn't think of that. I'm so stoked to be on this gorgeous island, I don't want to miss a moment of the daylight. And yes, totally out of my pattern as a musician. Something about the air here, I guess. I'm raring to go, which is why I called. Want to go on a bike ride with me to this place called Arch Rock I read about?"

"A bike ride? I haven't ridden a bike in a long time …"

"No problem. I have a tandem bike reserved. You know the ones you ride together with the pedals in the front and the back? The concierge set one up for me, and I thought you might like to be my backseat driver for this adventure," he says.

"That sounds amazing, and I think I can handle the back peddling. You aren't going with Vivian?" Maybe I shouldn't have asked that.

"Oh, she said something about a shopping trip or something. She's not around. What do you think? Are you up for a bike ride in an hour? I'll bring some snacks, and we can stop for a picnic somewhere on the journey."

"You sound like a school kid on the first day of vacation! Yes, I'll be ready. Where do I meet you?"

"You said it perfectly. I feel like a school kid ready for fun. Meet me down by the pool house. That's where the bike will be. Sorry it is so early, but I have a call with my label this afternoon I have to take. And, then we have practice after dinner. Full day, but why waste a minute, right?"

"Your enthusiasm is catchy. Okay, seven a.m. sharp by the pool. I'll be there. Don't leave without me!"

"See you then, Alice!"

A whole morning with J.D. and then I'll still have time to stop at The Creative Lilac to meet Sister Mary-Margaret. I don't care if I skip dinner. I can fit it all in.

Quick shower, jean shorts, a light blue t-shirt, and my sweatshirt just in case. I'm not going to let my mind freak out about riding a bike, but I hope I remember how. It's been a few years, but then the saying goes … it's like riding a bike. We'll see. I don't want to be late. Just a little lipstick and blush, mascara. Who am I kidding? I want to look good, at least as good as possible when it comes to this face. The fact he wants to spend some time with me is causing that pounding feeling again. He must like my company. He must like — *stop, Alice!* It's a bike ride. Don't blow it up to be something it isn't. I can't wait to see him, alone.

A glorious day! Not a cloud in the sky, cool brisk morning air, the dew is still on the grass as I cross the lawn toward the pool house — oh, God, you made a beautiful day!

"Milady!" J.D. says with a bow. "I picked up that saying

since I've been here. I like it! Ready for some fun, Alice … milady?"

"Yes, I am. I hope I can keep up. Like I said, it's been a while since I rode a bike."

"Oh, you'll be fine. It will come right back to you. I think I know where we are going, and there are some road signs according to the concierge. It's a trek, but we should beat the tourists because it's so early. I've got a camera in my backpack too. So here we go!"

Gesturing me to get on back, I hope he's right. With him keeping the bike steady, I can jump right into the rhythm as he starts pedaling. This is much easier than worrying about the balance and steering of riding alone, especially with vision in only one of my eyes.

I love these back roads. J. D. has somehow figured out how to skip the downtown streets. Oh, the colors as we whiz by — the trees in full bloom, the occasional horse on their way to a daily chore, and a few tourists out and about. This is freedom. I'm on a bike ride with J.D. Grayling!

Even up hills, he can really keep us going fast! And he's right. There are less people. As used to getting mobbed when someone recognizes him as he must be, I bet it gets old. A road sign — less than a mile to get to Arch Rock. Time stand still! I don't want this morning to end.

"You doing okay, Alice? I know it's hard to hear with me facing the other way," he says, turning back slightly. "I just want to get there as soon as we can."

"I'm doing great. I'm with you. Let's push it and get there," I say.

"Thanks, co-pilot. Here we go!"

He kicks it up a notch, and it seems like in a blink we are pulling into the little area around Arch Rock. Without the carriage tours started for the day, we have the place to ourselves. Perfect! Oh, this view! This magnificent rock with the blue sky oozing through the large hole. Climbing the little stairs and railing to get as close as we can to this wonder of nature, it's fun to watch J.D. click away on his camera.

"Now, from what I could learn, this is a limestone formation, but I like the story I heard about it better. Something about an Ojibwa Native American lady named She-who-walks-like-the-mist disobeyed her father and fell in love with a man of the stars instead of the suitors in her village. Her father punished her by bringing her to this turtle island and putting her here by this rock where her tears wore a hole while she waited for her true love. The stars shone through this hole. Her true love walked toward her and carried her up to the land of the Sky People. According to legend, the rock is still here to remind people of her story. That's paraphrased, and I'm not sure I even remember all the parts correctly, but it's something like that," he says.

"What a cool story. I never heard it before," I say.

"My favorite part is about finding true love and not settling for anything else," he says.

Could he possibly be hinting something to me?

"Here, you come over here, and stand right in front of this corner, and I'm going to back up and get a picture of you with the whole rock in the picture, too. Okay, hang on. There, that looks good. Okay, a big cheese, and one, two, three," he says taking the picture. I can't believe he wants a picture of me.

"I wish we could both be in the picture," I say.

"Here, let me get back here and come in close, I'll hold the camera way out and snap it. I am kind of good at this from doing it with fans all the time. I imagine I don't always get everyone in the frame, but I think I'm better at it than I used to be. Someone should invent something to make this easier. Okay, get as close as you can. I'll put my arm around you and hold out the camera like this; get ready to say cheese again," he says.

I move in close to his face as he holds out the camera. Am I smiling for the picture or because I don't want this moment to end? I love being this close to him.

"There. I must have at least one good picture! I'll have to see what they have for film processing on the island. Maybe they have one of those camera places that can do it quickly, or someone can run it to the mainland. I don't want to wait until the end of the summer to see these beauties with this beauty in the picture," he says, giving a little tickle under my chin.

Whoa. I might faint at Arch Rock.

"You mean the beauty of Arch Rock," I say before I can stop myself.

"Oh, it's beautiful, but so are you. Never forget that Alice," he says. "Look at that view of Lake Huron down below. Even the stones on the bottom are easy to see, it's so crystal-clear. Amazing! I'm so glad I got to see it with you."

"Thanks for thinking of me. It really is breath-taking. I love the story you told, too. It's fun to think about."

"Yes, a rock formed by true love. Way more interesting than a geological explanation, right?"

"Absolutely. I think we came at a good time, because here come more people," I say, noticing there is some pointing going on from a small group that arrived while we were lost in the moment.

"And that's our cue to vamoose, right? Let's hop back on the bike and head toward the inland side of the island. I heard people talking about tons of forget-me-nots, and if I observed correctly, there was a certain lady with those favorites of mine embroidered on her shirt the other day,"

This man doesn't miss anything!

"You noticed that? Yes, they are my favorite, too. I love them, the blue, so delicate," I say.

"I think they perfectly match the blue in your eyes," he says. "Come on. I'll race you to the bike."

Giggling at how fast he takes off, I'm trying to keep up. Hopping on, more people are coming up the path, staring and pointing. At least I know when I'm with him, they aren't looking at my face. They are looking at him. I could be invisible, unless they are wondering why this famous guy is with this below average girl. I can't help it; I need one last look as we leave. Maybe I can get one of the pictures he took of us. Even if I don't, I'll remember this forever.

Whizzing down one path, and turning onto another and another, I have no idea where we are. J.D. seems to know where we are headed. And there they are! The ground is covered with the vibrant blue everywhere we look, enfolded by a forest.

"Let's stop here, Alice. There's no one around and I see a little area where we can sit down and have a snack. All that pedaling made me hungry. This is perfect. We'll be right here with our favorite flowers," he says slowing down getting ready to stop.

"It couldn't be more perfect or beautiful! Look at their lovely little blue faces reaching to the sky with the yellow sunshine accents. Aren't they glorious?" I ask.

J.D. takes off his backpack and pulls out a canteen, two tin cups, and a plastic bag filled with Gorp. Sitting down in a patch of grass next to the flowers, he pours from his canteen.

"Sorry I don't have something better, but I knew I could only carry so much. Do you like trail mix?" he asks.

"Trail mix? So, that's what you call it? We call it gorp in my neck of the woods," I say.

"Gorp? Where did that name come from?" he asks.

"I've heard two theories on that. Good Ole Raisins and Peanuts — that stands for Gorp, or Granola, Oatmeal, Raisins and Peanuts. But I first learned it as gorp. No matter what you call it, I didn't have breakfast, so I'll take a big handful. It looks delicious" I say.

"That's because you had a crazy guy waking you up at the crack of dawn to go for a bike ride. Who had time to eat?" he says with a big laugh.

"This is beautiful and the most fun I've had in a long time. Thank you for thinking of me, J.D."

"I've been thinking about you a lot lately. How you play

instruments and know my songs so well has blown me away. Really. I've never seen anything like it. I can't believe you haven't been around playing on people's albums in Nashville or L.A."

"Ha, that's funny. That doesn't happen to girls from Cheboygan, Michigan who look like I do."

"Alice, really, you are beautiful. It makes me feel sad you don't know it. Did you have to wear a patch since you were a little kid? Is it something to do with your vision?"

"No, I was 'normal', as they say, until I was seventeen and graduating from high school. I was in the car with my mom, and we had an accident. I guess I'm lucky to be alive, but half of my face didn't make it. I don't have any sight in that eye and, well, you see what I look like. I'm very self-conscious of it. It doesn't seem to be such a big deal to people since I've come here, but I lived with my uncle after my mom passed a few years ago. He made sure I knew every day that I am basically some kind of freak. My face has been my focus. That's why I spend so much time learning every instrument, it took my mind of me. My uncle owned the music store where I grew up, and now he's selling it and moving on. That's why all the instruments will go to an auction house in Nashville to be sold. Which reminds me, he made me promise to get them all signed if you wouldn't mind," I say.

"No problem. We'll have the whole band sign them."

"That would be great. Thank you."

"Let me tell you what I see when I look at you. Genuine beauty and talent. An authentic person. You wouldn't believe how hard that is to find these days. I dwell in phonies. It becomes lonely wondering who wants to really know you or wants to use you for something."

"Well, thank you. I'm flattered and humbled that you would say something so lovely to me. I've been an admirer of yours since I discovered your first album, but of course, it wasn't the real you. It was the guy on the album cover," I say.

"Oh, that guy. Yeah, he's something else," he says with a laugh.

"It's been awesome to see that you are an exceedingly kind, sincere, authentic person yourself. And I do love your music. Your writing touches something deep in my soul — like if I could write a song, that is exactly how I wish it would turn out, if that makes any sense!"

"We should write a song together. With your musical know-how, it would have a fantastic melody and you don't know if you can write lyrics until you've tried. Maybe I'm Bernie Taupin and you're Elton John," he says, refilling my water cup.

"I'd love to try if we ever get that kind of time. That would be so cool," I say.

"Would you do me a favor, and stop thinking about your face as something to hold you back? You had an accident and you're alive. That's what is important. You're a beautiful, extremely talented, very gorgeous woman. That's how I see you," he says.

"That might be more than I could think about myself. Such sweet, encouraging words that I will never forget coming from you. I mean, how can I ever forget, among the forget-me-nots?"

J.D. leans over and kisses me on my cheek. Not the good cheek. The cheek under the patch. Please, time, stop right now. I will never have a better moment in life than this one. This kiss on the cheek — so gentle and not coercive in anyway. Pure sweetness. Savoring the moment with silence, we both are jolted back into reality as an out-of-control, group of giggling teenage girls almost plow into us.

"Whoa," J.D. says as we're laughing so hard, we can barely speak. "I can read the headlines now. Killed among the forget-me-nots by ne'er-do-well teenagers off on bike rampage."

"Stop! I'm going to start laughing again, and my ribs already hurt," I say.

Putting all the things back in his backpack, he steadies the bike so I can climb on.

"I wish we didn't have to head back. I could spend all day out here, but I can't miss this call I have coming up. Darn! Who wants to do business on such a fantastic day?" J.D. asks.

"I agree, but since we are heading back, would you mind dropping me off at The Creative Lilac. You know the store where we met? I promised Piper I would meet her friend Sister Mary-Margaret who is in town. I mean if it's not too hard for you to ride it back without me?"

"That's no problem. They said I could bring it back to the pool house or drop it at any of the bike shoppes in town. I'll do that and jog back up to The Grand in plenty of time for my call. Since I won't be taking much time to say goodbye when I drop you because of, well, you know how people act. Let me say my goodbye now. Alice, you have been the best bike co-pilot a guy could ever hope for, and I can't thank you enough for spending the morning with me, milady," he says.

"I had the most fun, probably ever, and I'll treasure this little adventure, always. And, if you do get a picture of Arch Rock with us, I'd love a copy. I'll be your co-pilot anytime. I honestly don't know if I could do the single bike thing, but the tandem is perfect."

"Speaking of which, let me put the bike down for a minute while I catch some pictures of you with the wildflowers behind you. The sun is perfect, and your eyes are reflecting the blue in the flowers — wow, Alice! Gorgeous! No wonder your last name means 'wonder' in French!"

"It does? I never knew that!"

"Yes, Alice Wonder, you live up to your name, milady," he says clicking away with his camera. "And, last one will be with me getting both of us in the picture ... and there! Can't wait to see these. Really, I mean it. Thank you for this incredible morning with you."

Another kiss on my cheek and drat. Here comes more bikers. It's time to go.

"To Oz?" I ask.

"To Oz!" he says as we hop on the bike.

Then we sing "We're Off to See the Wizard," all the way into town until we get to the more crowded section when we have to concentrate on biking and not calling attention to ourselves. Pulling up to the area in front of The Creative Lilac, he stops the bike and I hop off.

"Well, Miss Wonder, that was wond-der-ful, you are wonderful, and I hope you have a wonderful rest of your day. Say Hi to Piper and Freddy and tell Sister Mary-Margaret I'd like to meet her someday. Get all those people comp tickets so they can come to a show! Now, I'll be gone before someone drops a house on me, too!"

Sigh. The man knows his *Wizard of Oz.* As he rides away, I realize I am hopelessly, helplessly in love with this man. And he is already spoken for by another.

CHAPTER NINETEEN

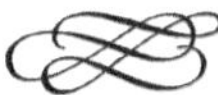

I love the now familiar little tinkle of the bell as I enter The Creative Lilac. Bijou and Labyrinth come running, and I pick them both up for kitty snuggles.

"Oh, you sweetie pies, how lovely to see you both today, you adorable kitties," I say.

"Miss Alice, so glad you could drop in. How are the art supplies working for you?" Freddy asks.

"Freddy, you know I've been so busy I haven't even opened the bag! But I can't wait for the moment when I have some time to play with the art supplies. Thanks again for getting them together for me," I say. "I think Piper is expecting me?"

"She sure is, along with Sister Mary-Margaret. Head on upstairs. They just went up for some tea. You came at a good time. It's been a busy day, but we are having a nice little lull right now, so I can get caught up on some things," he says, turning to the intercom and letting them know I'm on my way up.

Climbing the stairs, I feel a little nervous. I never met a nun, let alone had a conversation with one.

"Alice! I'm so glad you could get away and meet Sister Mary-Margaret!" Piper says, giving me a big hug.

"So nice to meet you, uh, Sister, um, Mary … I'm sorry. I'm not sure how to address you," I say. I clearly have no nun etiquette.

"Who does she sound like?" Piper asks, looking at the nun.

"If you want to be like Piper, the first time she met me, I think I remember her calling me, 'your nunness," Sister Mary-Margaret says.

They burst out laughing, and I can't help but join in. She's a tiny person, barely five feet if that, and still wears a habit.

"You call me whatever you want. Mary-Margaret is fine, or Sister Mary-Margaret," she says.

"Since Piper always starts with Sister, I will too," I say.

"Yeah, to me that's like your name — Sister Mary-Margaret," Piper says. "It's all one thought, although now that I think about it, I really should have stuck with *your nunness.*"

I love how light and fun they are. That anxious feeling I had is already gone.

"What would you like to drink? We're having some tea, but I think you'd like a cola?" Piper asks.

"Oh, that would be so refreshing. Sister Mary-Margaret, I'm surprised you wear a habit. I thought I read where most nuns stopped," I say.

"Yes, many have. But in Africa where I'm working, it's still common for nuns to wear a habit. I'm so used to it. Actually, it feels funny to me if I don't have it on," she says.

"That makes sense. Well, you look lovely. Thanks for the cold drink. I must look like a crazy mess. I've been out riding a bike all morning, and I am thirsty," I say.

"You were riding a bike all morning? Wow, you are ambitious," Piper says.

"Ask me who I was riding a tandem bike with all morning," I say with a wink.

"Get out! Are you kidding me? You were out riding with J.D.?" Piper asks.

"J.D. Grayling, the recording artist?" Sister Mary-Margaret asks.

"Yes, I didn't tell you, but he stopped in the store when Alice was here, and we all met him," Piper says. "Did I tell you she's the music tech for his shows this summer?"

"Oh, yes, you did mention that, but we've talked non-stop since I arrived, my brain has to catch up," she says with a giggle. It's easy to see why Piper likes her so much. There's something about her, something comforting and real.

"I like his music. I had a few of his cassettes. Good stuff," Sister Mary-Margaret says.

"He said to make sure to invite all of you to come for a concert when it works out for you. Let me know, and I'll get tickets for you, on the house, he said so," I say.

"That's awesome. I'll coordinate with Cam, and can Freddy come, too?" Piper asks.

"Yes, all of you, for sure. Another shocking thing happened. He overheard me playing some of the instruments and invited me to join in some of the numbers. So, I'll be adding a little harmony and be in the show," I say.

They squeal with glee, which makes me laugh again.

"Alice, what a few days you are having!" Piper says. "I'll make sure to let you know what will work. We can't wait!"

"I don't think any of that is a big deal compared to being in Africa. I'd love to hear more of your story, Sister Mary-Margaret. What do you do there?" I ask.

"Oh, I don't think it can live up to your great news, but it is rewarding to be there. I work in a mission with the poor. The need is great, especially in the slums. This is my first furlough, and I'm having a little bit of culture shock being back. Life here is so different, especially on this idyllic little island. But it's a nice break and will refresh me for going back," she says.

"I may not let her go," Piper says, hugging her shoulder.

"When you are doing what God laid out for you to do, you

have a peace through any circumstance that may not look like something attractive to someone else. He gives each of us just what we need to do the work He laid out for us. When you are in that place, you know it, and anything can feel right," Sister Mary-Margaret says.

"I did tell her about our conversations, Alice," Piper says.

"And I did read those Bible verses you gave me to read. In fact, I read them last night, knowing I was going to come here today. I didn't want to disappoint you," I say.

"I hope it wasn't a chore, but good news. What did you think after reading the verses?" Piper asks.

"I'm understanding to put my name in that one about God so loved me, Alice, that He gave His only Son, so I would have eternal life. Weird as it may sound, I never knew any of this before you told me about it. I need this. I am grateful for God's love to send Jesus. But I have some questions about the life that happens after. It sounds so selfish as I say it out loud, but what if God asks me to do things I don't want to do? For example, would I be expected to possibly go to Africa? That would scare me to death," I say.

"That's a fair question, Alice. But let's start with the love. You are saying yes to a Father who loves you more than anyone in life ever has or ever will. When He sees you after acknowledging and inviting His Son into your heart, He sees Jesus, not your sin. Everything in your life is for His glory and your good. Hard and challenging things still happen because we live in a fallen world. This isn't Heaven. That's ahead of us. But, with His great love, He takes everything and works it together for our good as it says in Romans 8:28. I find that many people have to think about God with fresh eyes. He's not just a superhero or superhuman. He is God, and His ways may not be our ways. That's a stumbling block for some people, but as you begin to open yourself up to who He really is, you'll be exceedingly thankful He doesn't think or act as we would. That would be a disaster in the long run, even if we would feel good about it in the short-term," Sister Mary-Margaret says.

"So, God is love. I guess I've always thought of Him more as someone who goes after evil and immoral behavior, and not all that interested in someone as inconsequential as me," I say.

"Every single person is as much a 'whosoever' as anyone who has ever lived. He is no respecter of persons; meaning, we are all the same. He's not interested in status, race, gender, none of it. We are all His children, and He loves us. He made a way through Jesus for us to reunite with Him. That's ultimate love," Piper says.

"He is perfect love. That's something that doesn't exist in human relationships, even between people who love each other. There will always be disappointments between people, even between great couples like Piper and Cam," Sister Mary Margaret says.

"Yes, I kind of had to learn that the hard way," Piper says, "Being newly in love and married, there was some definite friction when I put Cam in the role that only God, Jesus, and the Holy Spirit can have. We had a very rough first Christmas because of my unrealistic and misplaced expectations," Piper says.

"No person can ever fill up that hole in the heart, that place where we all have a yearning for perfect love. When we expect a person to fill it, sooner or later, we will be let down. We may think God has let us down when things don't go as we would wish, but when we look back at life, we will know, He never did. He can't. He sees the whole story that you are, including your happy ending, which is eventually living with Him forever in Heaven. That's what you're saying yes to when you say yes to Jesus. You are saying yes to perfect love — a love that casts out fear, as it says in the Bible. That includes the fear that He's going to totally make you live a life out of the scope of the giftings and personality He gave you in the first place," Sister Mary-

Margaret says. "I wanted to go to Africa. It matches with my heart's desire and my giftings and talents he gave me as an individual. And it was a gentle, clear nudge from the Holy Spirt that got me there. I didn't say yes to Jesus and get thrown on a plane. That's not how a loving Father works. Does that make it clearer?" Sister Mary-Margaret asks with a gentle smile.

"Yes, so helpful. I have looked at God through my limits. I see that now. And yes, that kind of looking at God is scary," I say.

"It's a relationship with Jesus, God, and the Holy Spirit, and like any relationship, it grows when you really get to know their character and spend time with them. That happens by reading your Bible and praying. So many people look at that as a chore, but when you think of it as a relationship with the greatest love, you approach it differently. You realize that even though day-to-day life has hard things, you have constant hope in the God of the universe who loves you," Sister Mary-Margaret says.

"The life of a Christian is challenging, but it's so fulfilling, and it leads to joy. Would you like to pray with us right now, and open up that relationship with your forever family?" Piper asks. "Feel free to be honest, but I would kick myself later if I at least didn't ask you."

"I'm not gonna lie; it's a lot to think about or understand, but I remember you saying we start out like little children, Piper. And I know that meeting you is not a coincidence, Sister Mary-Margaret," I say.

"There are no coincidences," they say together, gently.

"So, I've been told. I think I am feeling … ah, not quite sure how to describe it — drawn to do this, to say, yes. Is it the Holy Spirit, possibly? I can't believe I'm even saying those words," I say.

"Embrace the love that is indeed drawing you right now. Jesus is a gentleman, and He never forces His way into a heart, but, oh how He loves to be invited," Sister Mary-Margaret says as she takes my hand, and I take Piper's outreached hand.

"Piper, why don't you say a prayer, and Alice and I will reflect your words as we all pray together. There's nothing about these specific words, Alice. It's just using words from your heart to tell Jesus that you acknowledge He died for you personally, how you want Him in your life, you are sorry for your sins, and want to live for Him."

"Yes, let's pray right now. Dear Jesus, thank you for loving us enough to come and die for our sins. Forgive me of my sins. I accept You as my personal Savior and ask You to come into my heart," Piper prays, and we repeat her words.

"And Lord, give Alice your peace, your guidance, and show her each step of her walk with you," Sister Mary-Margaret adds. "And we ask this in in the name of the Father, the Son, and the Holy Spirit."

When I look up, I see her make the sign of the cross that I've seen people on TV do. The tears in their eyes match mine as Piper reaches for a tissue box.

"You are now a sister-in-Christ, and we are here for you, Alice," Piper says handing me a tissue with a hug. "You are part of God's forever family."

"Thank you. I'll never forget this moment. I know I'll screw up. What do I do then?" I ask.

"We all make mistakes. We are human. The Bible says to confess our sins. In other words, talk to Jesus. Acknowledge the sin to Him through your personal prayer and ask for forgiveness. When we do that, and mean it, we're told He removes the sins as far as the east is from the west and doesn't remember them anymore. So, what I like to do when I know I've sinned, or even if I wasn't sure and I'm getting a little tug on my heart — that Holy Spirit nudge or drawing — is talk about it right away with the Lord. I want to clear up anything between us as soon as I can. I mean, that's what you want in any good relationship, right? This is not about being perfect, but it is about our heart motives and our attitudes," Piper says.

"You'll get those little Holy Spirit nudges, those heart tugs, especially if you are paying attention and looking for them. Remember, this is all real. It's as real than what we know here in this world. You also have to be aware of the fact that the devil may try to throw you off track. That's why it's so important to read the Bible and hang out with other believers. You have to be intentional about living this life. But God won that battle at the cross, so call the devil out for who he is — a liar. Read the story of Adam and Eve in Genesis and see how the serpent, representing Satan spoke to Eve, very sly, cunning, and deceiving. Always remember as it says in 1 John 4 verse 4 — I'll paraphrase a bit, but greater is He that is in you — meaning Jesus and the Holy Spirit — than he that is in the world. Anything you're sensing that doesn't line up with the Bible can't be from God. It's not God's Spirit pushing you in that way. The devil does love to deceive, but when you are with God, you will start to see it. Don't be afraid to pray and ask God to make you aware of his deception. Always remember that you have the One who is greater and has overcome the deceiver," Sister Mary-Margaret says.

"And don't be overwhelmed by all there is to think about. Remember, you're starting as a little child, and each step will be clear to you as God leads you," Piper says.

"Well, let me say, I have never in my life had a conversation quite like this one, or learned so much in a small amount of time. But now I am His child, and I do want to read my Bible and understand," I say.

"I have Bible studies here in the studio, and there are multiple churches to attend. If you want to go with me and Cam, if you ever can on a Sunday, let me know," Piper says.

"And I'm at St. Anne's, and happy to welcome you at any time. Although, I am here for a brief time. You will be blessed wherever you want to fellowship with believers, that's for sure," Sister Mary-Margaret says.

"Thank you, both. I'll have to see what will work with our practice schedules for the band. I guess I have a confession I might as well get your advice on right away. I really have feelings for J.D., and he seems to like me, although he's also been like a great friend. He has a girlfriend already, but I'm wondering how I'm supposed to approach all these feelings?" I ask.

"Hmm, that's an intriguing question. The first thing you want to do is pray and ask God about what He wants in your life. In my experience, you don't get a big picture answer, you simply get the next thing. And if you don't have the peace in your heart that you'll come to recognize, then sometimes you wait, and you don't do anything until some clear direction comes either by something in the Bible or something someone says to you. God can communicate to you in all kinds of ways. Be listening," Sister Mary-Margaret says.

"And, it says in the Bible that believers belong with believers. Now there are many people married who come to God after they are married, and of course, they aren't supposed to run out and end their marriage. But Paul in the Bible has a lot to say about the strength of a marriage when you are both dedicated to God. Since you aren't married yet, don't let anything get too far with someone who isn't going to support or understand your dedication to being a Christian. And be careful of someone who says they believe just because they think that's what you want to hear. It's all shiny and pretty in the beginning, but when the honeymoon wears off, marriage is hard even for Christians. So, take that out of the equation, and yikes! It's really hard. I don't think you have to agree on everything, but you should agree on the fundamentals that Jesus died for our sins and rose again. Is J.D. a believer?" Piper asks.

"I have no idea, but I guess I've never heard him talk about God or faith, but then he's never heard me talk about it either," I say.

"You pray, and we will pray too. Don't take things too fast. Keep your friendship but be careful about how you let your heart and mind leap ahead in the romance department. As you said, he already has a girlfriend. These first feelings for someone can really send you on a wrong path if that's all you focus on. It becomes easy to rationalize what you should or shouldn't do. It's time to focus on your new relationship with Christ and let Him guide and lead you, because He has promised that He will. Be careful with those very strong feelings starting inside you. Feelings can get us into trouble. I know they have sent me down some bad paths, because I listened to the feelings far more than the truth," Piper says.

"Well said, Piper. We will be praying for you, for your new walk, your thoughts about J.D., and your future once your concerts are done this summer. Do you have commitments after that?" Sister Mary-Margaret asks.

"No, I didn't, and now, I really don't. I know I have to be committed to praying about where or what I'm supposed to do. J.D. mentioned doing some studio work in maybe Nashville or L.A., but that could have been him making pleasant conversation, not sure," I say.

"Well, we are told not to worry, but instead to pray. So, you have your assignment — read your Bible, daily is best. Read all of John and then try Matthew, Mark, and Luke. Let the Holy Spirit lead you and remember to read things in context. What was happening before and after, and what was Jesus teaching or the writer of that chapter saying? And that's where Bible study and church will be very helpful in learning, too. It's lifelong. Believe me, we never 'arrive' and know it all and say, good deal, I'm all set. That isn't going to happen. Every day we learn, we grow, we stumble, we ask for forgiveness, and we receive the perfect love that will never leave us forever and ever," Sister Mary-Margaret says.

"Do you talk about God all the time when you are together?" I ask.

"Ha! We talk about God a lot because Sister Mary-Margaret is great at helping me with my million questions, but we talk about all kinds of other stuff, too. And we try to watch *I Love*

Lucy together whenever we can. That's how we became friends, watching our favorite show," Piper says.

"Yes, sometimes I'm Lucy and she's Ethel, and sometimes I'm Ethel and she's Lucy, and we always have a good laugh with popcorn and treats. You are more than welcome to join us anytime for our laugh fests, too," Sister Mary-Margaret says.

"She's the one that showed me my need of Jesus, even though I grew up with a father who was a pastor and eventually a televangelist. It was all just 'show and tell' to me, not real. This dear lady opened up the gospel to me and showed me my need to love and forgive, especially those who had hurt me and didn't deserve it," Piper says.

"None of us 'whosoevers' deserve the love and forgiveness of God, so why can we ever hold it from another person? Jesus came to show us a different way to think and to live," Sister Mary-Margaret says. "Alice, your gifts in music, those are gifts from God. He is going to use you. He will use you right now where you are and in the future. I don't think you are called to Africa," she says with a smile.

Laughing with these two is like joy bubbling up from my toes to the tip of my head. It's so freeing, genuine, and it fills a longing I didn't even know I had. Friendship, true friendship with people who love you for who you are and want the best for you, enough to tell you about the best friend they ever had. What a treasure.

"I kind of feel like I've been living in a cave up until a few weeks ago, and the entire world is new to me every single day by learning something new. Thank God for the sunlight and I'm not huddled in a room in the back of a music shop anymore," I say. "Listen, I do have practice tonight, so I better hike on back up to the Grand. Piper, please call me with some dates that work out for all of you to come to a show, the sooner the better. I'm hoping I can introduce you to the band and J.D., for those who haven't met him yet. Then, of course, there's Montague, the manager. He has it out for me and is always excluding me or saying mean things when J.D. isn't around," I say.

"Well, keep doing the right things, and even though it feels like he's the last person you want to pray for, fit him in there. We are called to pray for our enemies and those who persecute us. God can turn around anything. Now truth be told, we haven't seen that yet in Katherine Sims-Dubois, but Cam and I grit our teeth and pray for her. With God's help, we'll get past the gritting teeth in those prayers at some point. God can do anything!" Piper says.

"Thank you again for the love you've shown me, and now I have to work on believing that some other 'big shoe' isn't going to drop, and this all isn't real. That's how my personality is, and I don't want to think that way anymore," I say.

"There's a story in the Bible, in Mark, chapter nine I think it is, where a man wants Jesus to help his son get rid of an unclean spirit in his life. The man asks Jesus, that if He can, will He please help the boy. Jesus tells the man to not approach it wondering if he can or not, that anything is possible with God. The man replied that he believes, but to please help him with his unbelief. And that's a lesson for us today. We believe, but we still have unbelief, and God can help us with that. This is real. Remember those feelings, though. When they come, speak truth to them. Feelings will be all over the place and mess with us, and as women, of course, we've got those lovely hormones to deal with too. But put everything into the light of God's truth. Don't rely on your old-style feelings. Rely on truth which you can always learn through prayer, guidance from other believers, and promptings — those nudges from the Holy Spirit," Sister Mary-Margaret says.

"Okay. I can't learn one more thing today or my head will explode," I say, giving them both a hand squeeze. "Seriously, thank you. Those words are so inadequate for all you've given me today. I should get going, and let me know about the concert, and I'll let you know about church or Bible study or whatever I can work out. And yes. Please pray for me. I'm going to need it," I say heading toward the stairs.

After goodbyes and one more hug, I run down the stairs with a pet for each kitty and a quick wave to Freddy who is busy checking out a customer. Stepping out into the late afternoon sunshine, it feels like the first day of my life. I guess it is. The first day of my new life. I feel like I could float up to the Grand. It's getting busier every day with tourists, and I'm sure many of them will be coming to the show. The tickets are selling out easily. How do I really feel about not just practicing with the guys but actually performing? Scared, Lord, I'm scared. Oh, I think I'm praying, Jesus, and talking to You. Yes, this feels right, and thank You Lord for saving me and making me a part of Your family. I sure don't deserve such a gift. Lord, I …

"You sure get out and about, don't you?"

Oh boy. I didn't expect to see her standing right in front of me with this wild look in her eyes. It's her alright, huge yellow daffodils on her skirt, and yes, daffodils on her shoes. But now, she has a parasol to match, and she's holding it up horizontally to stop me.

"Don't think I didn't see your little bike excursion, and don't think I will keep your little hanky-panky from dear Vivian. She will not be happy about it; you can bet your life on that!" Oh man, another encounter with Katherine Sims-Dubois!

"Can you walk with me, Katherine? I have to get back for practice," I say, pushing the parasol aside and starting to walk.

"Oh, back to spend time with J.D., huh? While the cat is away, the mouse will play —very sneaky. They are practically engaged you know, so you better watch your step around him."

"It was an innocent bike ride, not sneaking around. We were both free, and he wanted to see some of the island. That's all it was," I say. Why do I think I need to explain anything to her?

"Let this be your warning. I know everything, and I do mean everything that happens on this island. And I won't stand for you standing in the way of Vivian and her true love. She has had to deal with your type way too many times, and this is the perfect situation, er, man for her. So, you have been warned."

With an emphatic pound of the tip of the parasol on the pavement, Katherine gives me that look which reminds me of Montague now that I think of it. And just like that, she's gone, blending back into the crowd of tourists. I have to get going, or I'll be late. Wow, that first test came really fast.

CHAPTER TWENTY

Thank goodness I had a banana and muffin in my room. There's no time for dinner and my Gorp has worn off. Such an eventful day. I want to remember every moment, well except for Katherine. That encounter I could have done without. Brush my teeth, fix my hair, touch-up my makeup, and head for practice. I've never had so much time in my life when I wasn't thinking about my face or how other people perceived me with the patch and the scarring. I never even thought this was possible. Thank you, Lord, for a new life and a new beginning.

I thought I would be at practice first, but someone is playing in the room already. I hope it's … yes, it's J.D.

"Is it normal for the boss to get here before the help?" I ask with a smile.

"Alice. I was hoping you would be here a little early. I wanted to play this bridge for you on a song I'm writing, because I think you'll have some insight on how to make it better," he says.

"Okay, I feel super flattered right now that you think I could play anything that would be better than what you could come up with," I say.

"Seriously, grab a guitar. Let's see what we can come up with," he says.

Since he's on a twelve string, I grab a six string and a stool and sit down near him.

"Did you have a good rest of your day after the bike ride?" he asks.

"I had a, well, most interesting day. Some of it life-changing, some of it confusing, and let's just say, it's been one spectacular day for sure," I say.

"Life changing? Wow. I'll have to hear more about that. I had a fantastic morning, although I didn't care for my conversation with the label. I've chosen not to wreck my almost perfect day with anything about that," he says with his fingers starting to fly on the frets.

"You can tell me anything. I don't mind, really," I say, paying attention to the chords.

"Nope, gonna keep your day perfect. Here we go. Here's what I'm thinking, but it's missing something,"

He plays some very cool chords and jumps into a minor key I didn't expect.

"Oh, that's a twist. I like that a lot," I say.

"Do you? Good, I wasn't sure about it. Jump in anytime," he says.

Our fingers are both moving quickly from chord to chord, and I start to see what he means. There is one thing that isn't quite there yet.

"I think you need one more chord change, a complete stop, and then pick back in, like this," I say, showing him what I mean.

"I'm liking that. Do it again," he says.

As I play, I can't help but enjoy how intently he's watching me.

"That's it! That's exactly it! That's what I needed. I knew you would know the answer. Thank you. I'm going to put that in the song, and you, pretty lady, are going to be listed as a co-writer of this song when I'm done. It should be going on my next album," he says.

"You don't have to do that. Really. I'm happy to help, if you think I can add anything," I say, and I can feel my face getting redder by the minute.

"Alice, you have to see yourself for who you really are – a fantastic musician. Something unfortunate happened to you. It's something no one would want, but it has nothing to do with the real you, the essence of who you are. You need to let your light shine in the word," J.D. says.

"I'm trying J.D. It's all new for me. I've had way too many years to think about nothing but my face. I lived with an uncle who never let me forget my shortcomings. But after today, I see the world differently. I do. I'm just so new at it that I fall into what I've spent all these years feeling. You are a great friend. Thank you for today and for including me in your music, "I say.

"Of course. Listen, I know it's been a short time, but I'm loving getting to know you. You're the kind of friend I want in my life. And when it comes to music, you do have a future. You deserve to get rewarded for all the work you've put in."

"That means a lot coming from someone with your talent. I'd be honored to be mentioned on your album, thank you," I say.

"Do you have a boyfriend, Alice?"

Whoa. That was a question I wasn't expecting.

"No, no. I can't say I've ever had a boyfriend. This is my first time out of my sheltered life at my uncle's music store. I'm sure you have noticed I can be awkward and there's so much I don't know for someone my age."

"Honestly, you are a refreshing change from what I'm used to. But you do have to be careful. The music world can be a scary place. People will try to take advantage of you. At some point, you may not know who likes you for you, or if they have an ulterior motive. Unfortunately, mostly people want some-thing from you. I don't see any of that in you, but people could take advantage of your kindness. When you're at the top, there's always someone nipping at your heels, trying to take you down," he says.

"Does this have something to do with your call today? You seem pretty down about it," I say.

"Ah, I'm an old, seasoned bum in this business. I've seen so much of it, but yeah, what they talked about today really got under my skin. Who's on top of the charts, who is overtaking my place, blah, blah, blah. Sally and the suits — always about profits. But that's not for you to worry about," he says with his adorable smile.

"You and Vivian seem very happy." I can't believe the words that just came out of my mouth!

"Do we? Hmm. We met in Europe and she's kind of tagged along. She did push to get this gig here for the summer, which isn't something I normally do, or they normally do as I've come to understand. I was ready for something different, so I went along with it. She's a nice girl, but there's no future. I haven't quite found the moment to let her know, and with us being at her relative's place, it's awkward," he says.

"It seems like I've heard comments that you are serious." I still can't believe I'm saying these things to him, but today he became a person to me, not a rock star — a person I care about.

"Well, I'm not going in that direction, so I hope there doesn't have to be some kind of unpleasant scene while I'm performing here. I'm keeping it casual, and I hope she will too. I guess time will tell," he says with a wink.

"Anybody home?" Miranda peeks her head in. "Oh, you two! Didn't expect that. I have the snack cart all ready, and Alice, I made sure there's some juice since you don't like tea," she says. "Enjoy. I'll be back later to clean-up." She always flits in and out so fast.

"You don't like tea? How can you be Alice in Wonderland and not go to the Mad Hatter's tea party?" J.D. asks. "And think about it! You're now part of the Mad Hatter's band!"

"Ironic, huh? It's not that I don't like it; I just get an allergic reaction, so I don't drink it. Really, I don't drink juice either, but she's under the impression I do for some reason. I stick to water and coffee mostly."

"I steer clear of juice and stick mostly to water. The guys love the pampering we are getting here and see the juice and tea as some kind of perk. Most gigs it's cans in a cooler, so I'm glad Miranda is spoiling them," he says.

The guys must be in the green room. I can hear the hum of their conversation.

"Woo hoo, look at the snack stand tonight! Boy, Miranda knows how to put on the feed!"

It sounds like Doogey, Jammer, Strings, and Bongo are all drooling at the snack table.

"Shall we join the motley crew for a snack and practice?" J.D. asks, gesturing toward the door.

"Absolutely, and since I skipped dinner, I'm pretty happy about the snack table tonight, too," I say.

They all seem surprised to see just the two of us come out of the music room and into the green room.

"Hey guys, look at the spread!" Bongo says.

"You are really trying to fatten us up," Strings says.

"You? You could use it, skinny guy," J.D. says giving him a small punch in the arm.

"Chow down, fellas, and let's hit the stage. I can't wait to see how Alice is going to wow us tonight," J.D. says, beaming at me.

"Alice, that mandolin part you added in 'Raincheck' blew me away. You can really play," Doogey says.

"Thanks, Doogey. I'm just trying to keep up with the guitar virtuoso you are," I say.

Such nice guys. The practice is amazing, and I can tell they are having as much fun as I am as I hop between the various instruments. Strings and Jammer pulled me over to a mic, so we could all do some harmony with J.D., and the three parts meshed with J.D.'s lead. When we were done with the last song, we all stopped and didn't say a word. It was simply perfect, perfect like this day. Putting the instruments back, we start to say our goodbyes for the evening with hugs all around. We have bonded.

"Alice, wanna take a walk on the porch?" J.D. comes close and asks me as the other guys are leaving.

"That would be …"

"J.D.! J.D! Surprise! I got back early from my shopping trip just so I could spend the evening with you, my love!"

Oh great, Vivian.

"Vivian! I thought you weren't back until tomorrow at the earliest," J.D. says.

"Oh, how could I stay away from my love for that long? You know how I miss you when we're not together my music angel," she says, grabbing him and nuzzling his neck.

"You two go ahead. I have some things to do," I say. I don't want to put any pressure on J.D., and he's in a bind right now.

"Yes, I had to rush back. After a phone call from some island friends, I just knew I had been away too long!" Vivian says, turning her gaze to me.

Ah, her look matches the one from Katherine-Sims Dubois. No mystery who made the call.

"I'll walk you to your room Vivian, but I have to get back to my room. I have a big day tomorrow, and I need some rest," J.D. says. "Great practice tonight, Alice. We'll talk tomorrow," he says with a wink my way.

"Yes, Alice, we'll talk tomorrow," Vivian says as I see her jaw clenching as she turns to deliver another look my way as they are walking out of the room. Lord, what is this talent I have for making enemies on this island?

CHAPTER TWENTY-ONE

I am happy about this decision. I start everyday by reading something out of my Bible. There's a ton I don't understand, but I am willing to learn. I know this is real, and it's something I've been missing my whole life. I skipped around and found in the book of Luke, Chapter 8, where Jesus tells the story of what happens to the Word of God, comparing it to a seed. When some people hear it, it falls on rocky ground and doesn't take root. Some falls on thorny ground and gets choked out, like how people let life's problems or pursuits stop God from being first in their lives. But, when the seed goes into good soil and takes root and grows, it produces beautiful things. I can tell how easy it would be to not be the good soil, and that's something that Piper and Sister Mary-Margaret have both made clear. I have to stay in-tune with the Bible and listen for the Spirit's leading. I know me, and old me could blow this off if I'm not careful. But I'm a new creation now, so Lord, keep watering my soul. I desperately need You! Sister Mary-Margaret also said it can't be all about emotions. Yes, they can be there, but the real walk isn't about emotion. It's about following what has been laid out for believers and walking by faith, not by sight. Read the Bible, pray, be with other Christians

... and something I can't stop thinking about. Does J.D. believe in God and Jesus? I've never heard him mention anything. He seems like a truly good person, but my eyes have been opened up to so much more than what I thought before. The weeks are starting to fly by way too fast, and I haven't had the time alone with him that I'd like to bring it up. Every night it's a new crowd, and they all love the music. I'm feeling like such a part of this group. It's helped to simply stay out of Vivian and Montague's path as much as I can. It seems to be working. Gosh, why do I jump every time someone knocks on my door or the phone rings?

"Hi, can I help you?" I ask the gentlemen at my door.

"Milady, I was asked to bring you this note," he says.

"Thank you for bringing it," I say with a smile. How nice is that to bring a note to my door? Even though I know tipping is not a practice here at the Grand, it's really hard not to give someone who goes the extra mile a little something, but I'll stick to their rules.

Alice,

Something has come up, and we need to start practice much earlier today. You may

already have plans; but if you can, please be at practice at noon. It's really important.

Thanks!

J.D.

Hmmm. Maybe he wants to break in an entirely new song. We have everything else so down pat. That must be it. I was going to see Piper today, but duty calls. Duty? To spend more time with J.D., hardly a chore! My pleasure is more like it. Besides, Piper, Cam, and Sister Mary-Margaret are coming to the show tomorrow night, so I can see them after the perfor-mance. It took some wrangling with all their schedules, but we finally settled on a night they could all come.

Okay, Lord, that's it for our Bible time today. I have to jump in the shower, get dressed, grab a little something to eat, and be ready for practice. Thank You for today. Show me what to do each step of the way. In Jesus name, Amen.

And yes, I will wear my shirt with the forget-me-nots which should help J.D. remember our lovely bike ride through those glorious flowers and woods a few weeks ago. I'm sure I think about it much more than he does, but I hope it's sticking in his mind, too.

~

"Oh, good. Thank you for coming early. I'm sorry to intrude in your time off, but I really need you here today," J.D. says as shuts the door behind me.

"No problem. What's up?" I ask.

"The guys are getting sick, one by one!"

"Like a flu or something?" I ask.

"It's weird. First Doogey called me last night. He was throwing up non-stop. A couple of hours later, Jammer and Strings gave a quick call that the same thing was happening to them. Then this morning Bongo also got hit with it, whatever it is. They all room together so it makes sense they would get the flu together, but none of them have a fever. It's really bad stomach pain, running to the bathroom with those issues — that sort of thing," J.D. says.

"Food poisoning?" I ask.

"Sounds like it, but they didn't have commonality in what they ate. They are really miserable, and I guess you can see, they won't be playing tonight," he says.

"They must be really sick, because I know they have that 'show must go on' mentality, like most performers," I say.

"Yeah, their current performance is saved for the rest-room and would not be suitable for any audience! So, it's you and me kid. Are you up for this?"

"Oh, wow. Just some accompanying instrumentals, or…"

"Monty is going to get the word out that we are pivoting to

some acoustic shows. He's billing it as an intimate night of music, hoping to not disappoint the current ticket holders before we can sell it that way for the next few days — hopefully shorter, but who knows?"

"Can they see a doctor?"

"Yes, they have a paramedic here on the island, but I've sent for a doc from the mainland. They may need to be hospitalized if they are losing fluids, but we'll know more after the doc sees them. In the meantime, will you play and sing with me for the next few shows?"

"Of course, I will! I don't want to disappoint you, I mean, a full band compared to just me …"

"You will do great. Do what you've been doing — hop in and do your thing. I'll try to give you a nod when I can. Pretend it's the two of us in a jam session, no one else is in the room," he says with that smile that melts my heart.

"If you think I can do it, I am willing to do all I can to make it great. But please tell me if you don't like something or it isn't going well, or something isn't working. I'll take a nod for that, too," I say.

"Don't worry. It's been so natural for us; this will be the same. There's no one I would rather have on stage right now than you. I know you will make me even better. Don't be timid. This is the time to let loose and share your music," he says.

"This is all so bizarre; I feel bad for the guys. Is there a flu going around the island?"

"That's what is weird about it. The small medical station here has no reports of any sickness, and from what Vivian could find out, there are no reports of sickness anywhere. That's why it's getting very suspicious, but then, why aren't you and I sick too?"

"I agree. If it's the flu, shouldn't we both have it? Or, I hate to say it, but maybe it's coming? Eeek, that's a terrible thought, but what if you can't play?"

"If I can't play, then you'll do solo shows until I can," he says.

I can't speak right now. Solo shows? Never!

"Alice, I'm kidding. Remove that look from your face. We would have to cancel the shows, but I don't want it to come to that. I guess for right now, be careful. Wash your hands a lot, get sleep, eat healthy … that's about all we can do," he says with a smile. He loves to tease me.

"Okay, no more heart stopping statements please. I think this is enough pressure for the moment," I say.

"Seriously, you will do great. So, shall we tackle this, and see what songs are going to work better now with this acoustic tactic? Obviously, there are a few we will drop, or if we have time, we take them from a whole new acoustic angle … could be interesting," he says.

"I'm glad you are so confident, and the spotlight will be on you. I'm happy to stay in the background. That's where I am most comfortable," I say.

"Follow my lead. Don't let anything freak you out. Just go where the music takes us, and I know the audience will love it," he says as we gather up a few instruments to move them on stage for practice.

"Not to bring up a touchy subject, but Vivian seems a little upset these past few weeks," I say, getting settled with my guitar.

"Yeah, she's been out-of-sorts or something. The whole thing doesn't sit well with me. Evidently, someone called her and told her we were off doing something and made accusations that you and I both know weren't true. We were simply friends having a bike ride, and someone, she wouldn't tell me who, was making a big deal out of it," he says. "Ever since then, she's been weird."

My heart is sinking at how he is describing it as "simply friends having a bike ride." I was hoping if was more to him.

"I guess on a small island, news gets around. I mean it was just a bike ride … no big deal," I say.

"Alice, it was a big deal to me. I loved spending that time

with you. I meant that it shouldn't have been a big deal in the eyes of anyone watching us ride by, that's what I meant to say. Truthfully, I don't know what to do about Vivian. Our relationship isn't working, to put it bluntly, but with her so tied to this island, and this gig, the last thing anyone wants is some kind of dramatic scene. I think I'm trying to keep things light and civil until the shows are done. We aren't compatible, I see that now. Our views of the world are vastly different. That's what I've come to find out in the past few weeks. I wish I would have realized it before I made such a long gig here, but I don't have regrets. If I wouldn't have come, I would never have met you, and that makes it all worth it," he says.

Okay, knock me off my stool because that made my heart sing.

"I'm so glad you are here," I say softly.

Oh, J.D., if you only know how I feel when I'm around you! I stop thinking about my face and my past, and there's only now.

"So, here's the songs I'm thinking of …"

As J.D. goes through the new order and his tips of what instruments I should play and where to add harmony, I'm half-listening and half daydreaming of a future together in music and life. I just don't know what he thinks about so many things, including God.

"So, will you agree with me that we can make this the best show ever?" he asks.

"Yes, absolutely, the best show ever. I believe it with all my heart," I say.

"Okay, let's go, one and two and …"

As we run through each number, he stops only if he has a suggestion for something different or a new angle. The songs really work. I don't think the audience will have anything to complain about with this new style. Full bands are amazing, but he is the draw, and this does cause a more intimate concert, for sure.

"Feeling good about everything?" he asks, coming over and putting his arm around my waist.

"I'm not going to lie, I'm really nervous, but yes. I can do this if I follow what you said. It's just you and me and a jam session," I say.

Turning to face me and cupping his hand under my chin, he tips my head up and looks me straight in the face.

"This audience is lucky; lucky, you hear me? They have the opportunity to see a beautiful lady with the most amazing musical talent I have ever seen perform. I love everything you are doing, and I mean that from the bottom of my heart," he says and plants a kiss on my forehead.

I can't say a word, only look into his face wishing the kiss had been on my lips.

"Now, go get a bite and rest up. In a short while, it's you and me on stage, babe!"

He called me babe!

Heading to my room, I know I just want a little something from room service. I couldn't eat a lot, nor should I with what's ahead. I need to chill out before I get ready for the performance. Better yet, I should stop at the lower café and get a half a sandwich to go, that might be easier. That's what I'll do. I love how this floor to ceiling chalkboard has all the days' meal specials listed. It makes it so easy to order. Let's see … something light. Oh no, look who is coming down the hall this way. It's Montague and Vivian — two people I don't want to see. *Okay, Alice, think.* Yes! Duck behind the big chalkboard, and they won't see you. Oh, great, this is where they have to stop and have their conversation, right in front of the sign!

"I'm so glad we are on the same page when it comes to her, such a snively little conniver. And now, finding out she's trying to steal your boyfriend!" Montague says half-whispering to Vivian.

"I know! I mean, it's apparent he's going to propose to me on this trip, and she's simply in the way. Oh, poor me, look at my face, look at my pirate patch! Please. Give me a break. It's like falling for a wounded bird, and she thinks it's something real. Idiot!" Vivian whispers back.

"She's going to get hers, don't worry. There will be some way to expose who she really is — someone trying to get close to J.D. and run the show. She doesn't fool me for one minute," Montague says as they both start to move on down the hall.

As I move further back behind the sign, so they don't see me, I hear Vivian's last comment.

"Yes, let's see her little sweet demeanor when she gets what is coming to her."

Lord! Please protect me from whatever they have planned. I don't know if I should tell J.D. any of this. I don't want to add to the pressure of this day. I'll see how the show goes tonight and then decide. Ugh, these two are the worst. And, Lord, I'm supposed to love my enemies? I'm not feeling it, not one bit.

CHAPTER TWENTY-TWO

This performance by J.D. was pure perfection. He's always great, but tonight he had a little something extra. I couldn't see out into the audience very well, which I appreciated, but from what I could see, the crowd was speechless. There was a hush after each song, as if they couldn't believe their ears. When we did "Raincheck" as a duet for the encore, the crowd went wild.

I'll never forget this for as long as I live! There have been so many memorable moments in these last few weeks. Walking off the stage together into the side room, I can't stop staring at him, and he's staring right back at me. And at the exact same moment I'm hearing myself laughing at the top of my lungs, and he is too. It's a pure laughter, filled with joy, that is coming from deep inside me. He must be experiencing the same thing.

"You are beyond incredible! All those instruments, and your vocals — perfection! Thank you, Alice. I've performed all over the world for thousands of people, but this night was different. I won't forget it as long as I live. I absolutely love performing with you. It's like you know where I'm going to go musically before I even do. You really are something," he said.

"Well, I feel the same about your performance. It was amazing, irresistible, and I don't think the audience knew what to do with themselves; they loved it so much! Thank you for letting me play with you and trusting me to help tonight. I'll never forget it either," I say as we move closer to each other, applause still ringing from the crowd as they are filtering out from the auditorium.

"Alice, I ..."

"J.D.! Bravo! What a performance, sheer perfection!" Montague says, bursting through the door with Vivian.

"Darling, my love, what a night. You were marvelous! My uncle was beaming after your performance. The Grand audience is just elated! Oh, J.D., I love you!" Vivian says pulling him away from being near to me.

"Thanks so much, but I couldn't have done it without Alice. She made the show tonight," he says turning back to me.

"Oh of course, Alice was very helpful," Montague says with a side glance toward me.

"Yes, she adds things, doesn't she, but you stole the show! They all really loved it!" Vivian said throwing her arms around J.D. "Come on, my love. Let's go celebrate with a late meal and a walk in the moonlight. Isn't that a great idea?"

"Actually Vivian, I need to work on some more music tonight with Alice. Monty, what have you heard about the guys? Are they improving?" J.D. asks.

"No, it seems they are all just as sick. The doctor is going to contact you in the morning. He's keeping an eye on the situation and waiting to see if they need to go to the hospital on the mainland," Montague says.

"J.D., really, you need to relax. Surely you can take a break for a walk with me. I'm sure Alice needs to go rest. She must be tuckered out, poor thing. I mean her face must hurt after so much singing," Vivian says.

"Why would her face hurt? Vivian, really, that's a weird thing to say. Listen, Monty, you keep me up to date on the guys, and Vivian, I'm going to have some dinner brought in for Alice and me while we work on tomorrow night's show. Then we can rest a lot tomorrow before the performance. We can take a walk tomorrow, I promise. I just need to stay with the music while the moment is here. Is that alright with you, Alice?" J.D. asks.

"Sure, whatever works for you," I say to J.D. while the two vipers glare at me.

"Oh, alright, as long as it's just music! No hanky-panky, right? I mean, it's Alice … after all," Vivian says.

"Again, Vivian, not sure where you're coming from sometimes, but listen, you two go along. Monty, no autographs tonight. We have a lot of work to do, and we need to concentrate. I'll catch up with both of you tomorrow. Let the musicians do their thing," J.D. says, pushing them both out the door. I can't help but smirk a little as I see her trying to grab a kiss while he just pushes her away, closes the door, and locks it.

Hearing them stomp away, he turns and looks at me as he comes closer.

"Now, Alice, where were we before we were so rudely interrupted?"

CHAPTER TWENTY-THREE

That kiss rocked my world. He kissed me so gently and told me he was starting to think of me as more than a fellow musician. We didn't even think about food or talk about the next set list — we just hugged and held each other. At that tender moment, words seemed inadequate for what I felt, and I think he must have felt the same.

"I'm sorry. I didn't even order us dinner. I wasn't able to think about food. Are you hungry?" he asks.

"No, I wasn't hungry anyway. The time with you alone was what I needed," I say.

"I know there's a lot to talk about, and I'm not worried about the show tomorrow if we are doing another acoustic one. You will shine again, no doubt. I just couldn't go another minute without letting you know that I am feeling so many things for you," he says, stroking my hair. "Can I walk you back to your room?"

"Yes, that would be nice, J.D.," I say.

We walk in silence, taking small sideway glances at each other and turning away in affectionate smiles. All too soon, we're at my door. I don't want him to leave.

"I've really enjoyed getting to know you, the real you, not

the guy on the poster. I hope you feel like you know the real me. I wouldn't want you to think I'm something I'm not and be disappointed," I say. "But the real me has come alive since being here."

"I want to get to know you better, much better. That's why I had to say something," he says, holding my hand. "I want us to be real with one another."

"I want that, too. This might seem like an odd question, but do you believe in God?" I ask.

"God? Like the man upstairs, say your prayers, God?"

"Yes, God, His Son, Jesus … what do you believe?"

"Now that was not a question I thought you were going to ask. Um, let's see. I think we should all be good people. God has a place, but for me, I'm not sure. I think Buddha and all the rest are all ways to God. If people just love one another, that's where it's really at. It's all about love. I think God kind of oversees that. I think He's in nature, in the sunrise, the sunsets, and the beauty all around us. I'm not an organized religious person, if that's what you're asking," he says with an inquisitive look.

"I'm not into religion either, but I have recently become very aware of God and a relationship. And I just wondered what you thought," I say.

"Well, my little philosopher, we will have to explore this big question further when we get time, but now, I need to go see what the docs are saying about the guys. I'm getting really worried about them, and I feel responsible for what they are going through, although I'm not sure why. Do you mind if I say goodnight now and go see what's happening?"

"Of course. I didn't mean to keep you. I hope they are better. It sounds miserable. Thanks for walking me to my room. If you find out anything or if I can help, let me know," I say.

"You're doing so much by helping me keep the show going and just by being you. I feel so encouraged when I see you, to know you are willing to give so much to the show, and well, to me," he says hugging me again. "Good night, Alice. Sweet dreams." And with another sweet kiss he is on his way.

With each button I close on my PJ's and then falling into bed, I feel super happy but also a little disappointed. I scared him away. He doesn't know God, not the real God. He's never heard the truth. He's as lost as I was. I have to talk to Piper and Sister Mary-Margaret about this. I don't know how it works. Can't two people, truly in love, be in a meaningful relationship and not agree about God? That should be okay, right? *Sigh.* I don't think I want to know the answer.

CHAPTER TWENTY-FOUR

Ahh, Mackinac Island. Even the cloudy and rainy days are beautiful here, but when the sun pops through my window, I know it will be a day bursting with color. I never used to think about the sun, the moon, or nature at all, but now I do, often. It's like a silent but ever speaking soundtrack that enhances each day. To think this all was created — God, You made all of this! You took some extra special care when You thought of this island, didn't You?

Life. J.D. It's no wonder that in every twilight half-awake, half-asleep moment throughout the night, I thought about you and how much I love you. Something real is happening between us, and it's different than the type of feelings I've had admiring someone from afar. I need to talk to Piper and Sister Mary-Margaret today, the sooner the better. I'll skip my Bible time this once. But I can't skip breakfast. Living on love and skipping meals will only go so far. I need my energy. What we put out for that audience on stage takes more strength and stamina than I would have imagined. It's an adrenaline rush, but afterward, my energy plummets —

unless I get to be alone with J.D. Then it pumps right back up! If the guys are having food poisoning, maybe not eating *is* a good thing. Still, no one at the Grand seems ill. They would have told people. Did they eat somewhere else with tainted meat or something? Why are they all so sick? None of it adds up. I hope J.D. gets word to me if he finds out something. Poor guys. Lord, help them.

Quick shower, I'll get ready fast, and yes, the more I think about the thick bacon, perfect eggs, and luscious toast spread with butter, I am starving. If this were a contest, I would win for being the first one in line at the dining hall, ready to chow down. Ha! No line. It's too early. The fudgies are all sleeping in. Fudgies — what a nickname for island tourists. I'm going to be a fudgie soon, too. Ugh, don't want to think about that.

"How many?" the gentleman host asks. How early does this staff have to get up to have everything prepped and ready for the guests? So much dedication to make this place run like a well-oiled machine.

"Just me. One, please," I say.

"How about one of our lovely tables by the window, so you can see the day come alive?" he asks.

"That sounds perfect," I say. He gestures me toward to a little table by the window looking out on the porch.

I devour the eggs, bacon, toast, roll with rhubarb jam, cottage cheese, coffee, and a big glass of water. I guess I was famished! *Slow down, Alice.* You have a show tonight, and you have to fit into your clothes.

"Well, someone is up and at it early!"

Ugh. Her sing-songy voice. Gazing at the Straits with this lovely breakfast made me drop my guard from whomever could sneak up on me.

"Good morning, Katherine."

Well, what is today's outfit? Let's see — fluffy skirt filled with, what are those? Turtles! Yes, she has turtles on her skirt, and wait for it, yes! Green pumps. She probably couldn't find shoes with turtles, but then where does she get the things she wears? Oh, the island is shaped like a turtle, so that's her theme.

"I'm meeting some of my group for an early morning meeting, and then I spotted you," she says.

"Yes, I have a busy day ahead, so I'm getting going," I say. I don't know what to say to this person. I'm sorry she even noticed me.

"Well, you might be interested to know that I know you will be performing tonight with J.D., odd as that is. I have front row seats, no thanks to you," she says, turning her nose up.

"Yes, I will be performing with J.D., and I'm happy you were able to get some good seats. It should be a nice show," I say.

"Montague, via Vivian, provided me with the tickets. I was hoping to see the whole band, but I guess this will have to do. It works into my schedule to come tonight. Terribly weird about the band being ill," she says.

She really does know everything that happens on this island. But of course, Vivian is her pipeline of information, the island snitch.

"It is terrible, and I'm hoping they all recover very quickly," I say.

"Do you? Or is this the opportunity you'd kill for, uh, and I *do* mean to use those words," she says.

"Katherine, are you saying I had something to do with the guys being sick? That's ridiculous!"

"Well, you've proven in the past that you will do just about anything to get J.D. to yourself, even though you know he is in love with someone else."

I'm so glad the restaurant is not crowded so no one else is hearing this stupid conversation. She won't shut up.

"Time will tell, won't it? The truth has a way of coming out, that's been my experience. With my love for this island, and my history of being a lifelong islander, I simply won't stand for anyone being here who causes harm in any way to anything that takes place on our little piece of paradise. It's always been my job to root them out and get rid of them. And, I might say, I'm exceptionally good at it."

Oh, Mackinac Island, how have you survived with this piece-of-work at the helm? Why don't the townspeople see her for what she is? Phony-baloney!

"Listen, Katherine, if you are good at it, then you should know you are putting your efforts in the wrong place. I have no ill will or anything to do with any insinuations you're making. I don't appreciate you accusing me of horrible things I would never do."

"I think she doth protest too much, and oh, what a tangled web we weave …"

"Who's weaving a web?" We both jump at J.D.'s voice as he comes up behind Katherine. He gives my hand a squeeze and winks at me, but all I see is the look on Katherine's face at his affection.

Her expression completely changes when he looks toward her.

"Katherine, so good to see you," J.D. says.

"Oh, J.D., you remembered my name. I'm flattered," Katherine says with that snake-fake smile she must have borrowed from Montague. "I was just telling our dear Alice here how much I and my friends are looking forward to your concert tonight. I do hope your band members are on the mend?"

"I'm happy to report that after a doctor visit and some medicine, they seem to be improving, slowly. Sadly, not fast enough to perform, but they are getting better. The doctors did some tests and sent them out. He has some suspicions about what they actually have, so we will all be relieved to find out more about that," he says.

"Testing? That seems a bit extreme for a flu, don't you think?" she asks.

Her cheeks are turning red, and this time there are no flowers on her skirt to match the color.

"Oh, routine, I guess. The doc wanted to be thorough. Have you heard of a flu going around?" he asks.

"No, no flu. But then it has to start somewhere, don't you

agree? Well, at any rate, I can't wait to see you perform tonight, J.D.," she says.

"Let me assure you, this will be an exceptional performance with the one and only Alice showing her talents. You won't be sorry you are here tonight," he says turning to me again with that smile and wink that makes me weak in the knees.

"Uh, yes, I guess. I'm sure all eyes will be on you, after all, you are the ce-le-bri-ty!" She couldn't help but sing that word. "I would never put myself on your level of course, but I do know a bit about being adored by constituents. It's all part of being the chairwoman of the Mackinac Island Town Board. It comes with the ter-ri-tory," she says, singing the last word again. "Perhaps you and Vivian and I can go out for a cool drink after the concert? I know how you love to spend time with her. You're such an adorable couple," she says.

"Thank you for the invite, but there is always much to do after a concert, so I'll have to decline. Perhaps another time," J.D. says. "I have a question, Katherine. Are those turtles on your skirt?"

"Why yes, yes, they are. Thanks for noticing. I go to great lengths to have my clothing reflect my love of the island, and since, as I hope you know, the island is shaped like a turtle, I had to commission this stunning frock. Heaven knows there are no stores sophisticated enough to carry such a lovely item," she says with a swirl of the skirt.

"Truly unbelievable, that's the best way to describe your taste in clothing," he says with a slight bow.

I may lose my breakfast right now from holding back the laughter.

"I know. I get complimented constantly. It's just a small thing I do to show my love of my homeland. Well, I hope you dedicate a song to me tonight, J.D. I'll be listening for that!" she says turning with a bigger swish and heading to meet her entourage toward the back of the room.

"Ta, ta for now J.D. ... and you, too, Alice."

Sitting down across from me, J.D. grins, and I'm just shaking my head over this whole encounter.

"There are really no words, are there?" I ask with a stifled laugh.

"There really aren't. Wow. What a way to begin the morning. But hey, isn't that great news about the guys? They're still quite sick but going in the right direction. I'm anxious to hear what the doctor tests have to say," he says.

"That is excellent news. Katherine sounded kind of weird when you said that tests were happening, but then she's the poster-child for weird, so I guess I shouldn't read much into that," I say.

"That's an understatement! I sure wish I was having breakfast with you this morning …"

"I don't have to rush. I can wait with you while you eat," I say.

"I would love that, but I'm actually meeting Sally Wagner for a quick meeting over breakfast, and Monty will probably join in too. They should be here in a few minutes. It's strange having someone from the label popping in and out of my business while performing, I'm not used to that. She's a nice enough lady but so focused on numbers. Always on my case about where I stand on *Billboard* charts, setting up label phone calls. I mean give it a rest, lady! I've never cared about any of that but leave it to the bean counters to obsess over. I've heard she's quite the task master from some other artists, but I've never had to be on her radar so much. Just my luck she had friends on the island and wanted to come along on this gig. At least I don't see much of her. Only when it's business related," he says.

"I don't envy you any of that side of the business. I just love the music. But, since they will be here soon, I think I'll duck out if you don't mind. Montague is not fond of me, and I'm not excited about seeing him," I say.

"Has he been treating you wrong? Really, tell me. I want to know," J.D. says.

"Let's just say, I'm not his cup of tea, and it's best when we avoid each other. Please don't say anything or do anything. Sometimes, personalities don't mesh, that's all. It's fine, really," I say, hoping he is convinced by my tone.

"He's something else — would be a great match for Katherine, actually. They deserve each other. Still, if he is unkind or there's anything you don't like, let me know. I know how to put Monty in his place. He tends to be overwhelming, and sometimes I wonder why I hang on to him, but overall, he gets the job done. What are you up to today before the show?"

"I'm going to see Piper and her guest, Sister Mary-Margaret, at The Creative Lilac," I say. "We have had some wonderful talks, and I need another one."

"Oh, so a nun, huh? Thus, your whole God-thing question. Is that where that came from?"

"I was wondering if that question bothered you last night. Well, we do talk about God, but that's a way longer conversation for another day. Right now, we both have places to be. Is the rest of your day filled up?"

"Yes, unfortunately, some publicity pictures, and more label stuff, so I won't see you until close to show time. But I can't wait. I know we will have a great show."

"Piper, Cam, Sister Mary-Margaret, and Freddy, remember him you met at the store? They are all coming tonight, so I'm super excited but nervous at the same time. I really enjoy spending time with them. They've become my friends, and I don't want to disappoint them in any way."

"Alice, you couldn't if you tried. You're a professional. I don't care how long you've been playing gigs; you are a true professional. The audience will adore you, just as I do," he says with another hand squeeze.

"You better be careful squeezing my hand in public. There are fans of Vivian's with eyes and ears everywhere. I'm not sure any affection is going to go over very well," I say. "I love getting to hold your hand or give you a hug in public, but this is getting messy."

I can't believe I picked this moment to be so honest with him, but something has to change.

"I know, Alice. I'm putting you in an unpleasant position. I promise, it's going to be handled very soon. I just have to think of a good way to do it so she saves face, and it doesn't become a 'thing' while we are still here performing, She, like Katherine, can be a force of nature when they perceive they've been wronged," he says. "I think she is capable of causing a ruckus that could be embarrassing for everyone."

"I can totally see that. But, yes, sooner than later. It's getting uncomfortable," I say.

"Hang in there with me. I have to get through the next few days, and then we have a break. It will all work out, I promise. I'll get it done, babe," he says, whispering the last part.

He always knows how to make me smile.

"Okay, well, I'm outta here. Don't work too hard. I'll see you tonight," I say.

I pray you are right, J.D. I pray it will all work out.

CHAPTER TWENTY-FIVE

I adore these walks to The Creative Lilac. At some point, I need to stop in some other stores, but with my limited time, all this window shopping has had to do the trick. Who can help but salivate with that sweet sugary aroma and the mesmerizing way they craft the fudge on the marble slab! Every single worker in their pristine white apron using the big paddle to keep turning the lava- like fudge over and over on the table makes me stop. Totally spellbinding! Good thing we are looking through their front windows, or we'd all be drooling in their delectable concoction.

I love watching the little kids' faces. It's all giggles and visual squirming when they think the fudge maker is going to miss the melting goo as it oozes toward the edge of the table. Their expressions are priceless. The squeal of delight when the escaping fudge is caught and brought back to the main log of goodness puts a smile on my face every time. I wonder if island people ever get their fill of this sweet decadence since they are here all the time, or is fudge a part of their daily food? Good thing I've stuck to my day-one decision to not partake except for the occasional sample piece. With all the delicacies at the Grand, there's already more food than anyone could wish for.

And the pecan ball! That first one made me almost fall off my chair! Whoever thought up a mound of vanilla ice cream rolled in pecans, served on a darling silver, chilled round dish, and then topped with Mackinac Island hot fudge and a dollop of whipped cream is a genius! Yes, a girl could put on a few "fudgie" pounds here in no time. All this walking, biking, and hiking are a necessary antidote. So many things that are only here in this special place.

God, you made all these people? Amazing. I wonder what stories each one will tell when they go home after their trip here. At least there's so much to look at, they don't notice eye patch girl. Funny. When I'm with J.D., I don't think about my face. I forget he has to look at it every day. One more reason I like him so much. He doesn't seem to care. I hope it's not true what the snakes have been saying — he likes me more because I'm strange looking. Ugh. Bad thought. I don't want any of those today, only good ones.

Here I am at my favorite place, The Creative Lilac. A little haven of hope and happiness for me. Thank you, welcoming tinkling little doorbell, a sweet way to welcome customers.

"Miss Alice! It's great you could pop in. We can't wait for the concert tonight. I have my best shirt all pressed and ready for the grand occasion," Freddy says, bounding around the counter to give me a hug. He's like the uncle I wish I had. For a guy who must be in his seventies, he's full of energy.

"Oh, Freddy! I'm nervous, but also super excited that you will all see the show tonight. It's a little different because the band got sick. You might hear too much of me," I say.

"Oh, even better! You are who I'm coming to see for sure," he says.

"That's sweet, Freddy, but you'll really enjoy J.D., I promise. Are Piper and Sister Mary-Margaret upstairs?" I ask.

"You betcha. I'll intercom you're on the way up," he says, pushing the button. "Miss Alice heading on up," he says gesturing me to head up the stairs.

Before he takes his finger off the button, I hear that now familiar happy squeal. Bounding up the stairs, I'm greeted with two big hugs.

"I can't believe you found time to see us on this momentous day," Piper says.

"Yes, you should be resting in your room, being fanned," Sister Mary-Margaret says with her endearing giggle.

"Ha, you guys are funny. I'm glad I get a moment with you both before I have to get ready for the show. I need some friendly faces, and I need some advice," I say.

"Well, have a seat my dear. You have come to the right place," Sister Mary-Margaret says, pulling out a chair at the table where we gather for our talks over coffee.

"We heard about the band members getting sick, so we have been praying for you, Alice. You must have to do more now in each performance. We've been praying for them, too," Piper says. "Are they getting better?"

"Yes, it sounds like they are still sick but on the mend. The doc who came took tests and is waiting for results. It's still a mystery. I hate to bring this up, because I have something more important to talk about, but I saw Katherine at breakfast," I say.

"I'm going to work hard to keep my lips sealed with any words right now. Watch me not talk," Piper says with raised eyebrows.

"She did enough talking for everyone. And her skirt had turtles, yes, you heard me, turtles!" I say. "But that wasn't the most disturbing thing. If I didn't know better, I'd say she was insinuating somehow that I had something to do with the guys getting sick so I could perform more, which is absolutely not true," I say.

"I'm still envisioning a turtle skirt, Katherine style, but why would she ever think you would have anything to do with the guys getting sick? I mean, really!" Piper says.

"I hope she didn't say that to anyone else to cause suspicion about me. She's angry because she saw me bike riding with J.D., and of course, she is close to Vivian. She's also making it clear they are a couple, and we are not," I say.

"Are you? A couple I mean?" Sister Mary-Margaret asks.

"Well, that's the real thing I want to talk to you both about. I know it's been a short time, but there's something special between us. It feels like electricity is shooting out of me when I'm around him, and not in a fan way, in a real way. We have connected through music and, well, as people I guess you could say. J.D. has let me know he has feelings for me and is only holding back from breaking up with Vivian to not cause a scene. He thinks it's awkward with her relatives owning the Grand, so he asked me to hang on a little bit until he can figure it out. Hearing myself say it out loud, it sounds like a stringing-along type of thing, but it's not. He's not like that," I say.

"How do you feel about him?" Piper asks.

"I'm falling in love, at least that's what it feels like. I don't have much experience in this department, that's for sure. Granted, everyone goes crazy over him, but this is different. I know what it was like to watch my mom get all giddy with a new man and then the fights they had when the relationship became more real. I'm not naïve to that," I say. "It's also a little different because I'm not seventeen anymore. I think this is love."

"That's what you're concerned about — you can't be in a relationship with lasting love from what your mom showed you?" Piper asks.

"No, I think Alice has a deeper concern," Sister Mary-Margaret says.

"Yes, I do. There's no question that I love him, and I would say he loves me. But I bluntly asked him about what he thought about God, and I didn't get the answer I was hoping for. As much as I would like to rationalize what he said, it's clear he's not on the same page. Now, I just got here myself, so I don't need to be judging anyone else. But before our relationship goes too far, how does that all work? I know I'm a believer, and I want to be one of the seeds that doesn't fall by the wayside. I'm committed to being one of the seeds that falls into good ground and keeps growing," I say.

"I'm impressed with your Bible study! That's fantastic," Sister Mary-Margaret says patting my hand.

"I'm trying to learn all I can. What does it mean when two people fall in love and one doesn't believe in Jesus? Does it matter? Can't we all just have our own beliefs, and before you answer, I know that's not right," I say.

"The Bible does talk about it actually, Alice. It's clear. Here, let me look it up. Yes, there it is, *2 Corinthians, 6:14. 'Do not be yoked together with unbelievers. For what do righteousness and wickedness have in common? Or what fellowship can light have with darkness?'* Sister Mary-Margaret says, showing me where it's at in the Bible.

"Unbelievers view the world differently than believers. The question becomes, how would that relationship affect your faith? If Jesus is the most important thing to two people, how does that affect every decision they make as a couple? If one has Jesus as the most important thing and one doesn't, can the believer really live the life they are called to?" Sister Mary-Margaret asks. "I'm not married, obviously, but I know marriage is hard. That's true even in a believer's marriage, a Christian marriage. Before you are too far into this relationship, you are wise to consider all of this. What do you think, Piper?"

"Your question shows so much maturity, Alice. It's hard when your heart goes crazy for that man you've been dreaming of. Cam and I were both brand new believers right at the beginning of our relationship. We didn't wait a long time to get married and in hindsight, we didn't know each other very well. I guess you could say we were both on our best behavior and didn't let the other see the 'real person' until we were into the marriage. And, sometimes, the real person scared the other person! Honestly, without the Lord, I wonder if we would be together. It's so easy to give up on a marriage. That's where the heart wants to go — the first impulse is to quit. I know it's not true in every situation, but I do think being on the same page in your faith walk is probably one of the most important keys to a long-lasting marriage. At our wedding, the pastor talked about a triple- braided cord from the book of Ecclesiastes. He told us how three cords are not easily broken. That third cord is Jesus. It's so true, at least from what I've seen about marriage," Piper says.

"I've seen marriages make it with two happy people going their separate ways in a faith walk," Sister Mary-Margaret adds, "but it's the minority, not the majority. And that's usually just a difference in the denominations they choose to pursue. Their core beliefs are similar. And here, before you are too far in, is the time to really examine your heart and pray. This is one of those times when choosing Jesus over what you naturally want could be extremely hard. I'm not telling you what to do, but it's clear The Spirit is giving you some nudges to pay attention. You can be very thankful for that," she says gently.

"Thank you both. I didn't have the details, but I know in my gut that being with a believer is what God would want. It makes sense. But, oh, how I've fallen in love with him! What if I tell him everything you told me, and he becomes a believer? That would be different, right?" I ask.

"With prayer and him deciding to make that decision honestly from his heart and not just to please or appease you, yes. It would be fantastic. But I've also seen so many people who told their dear one they believed, when they didn't. It was to stay with their mate. The proof is the fruit of their life, the choices they make, even if you aren't together. More time will tell if that person wants to follow Jesus, no matter what," Sister Mary-Margaret says.

"What if I wasn't a believer, married him, and then became a believer? God wouldn't expect me to get divorced, would He?" I ask.

"No, not at all. There are many verses that talk about a believing spouse being a witness to a non-believing spouse by how they love. But we come back to that same question: what will a life with a believer be as compared to a life with a non-believer? Which way would God ask you to go as you find yourself at these crossroads in life? The answer won't be based on any romantic feelings," Piper says. "I mean, I get it. He's gorgeous. He's famous. You've loved his music forever, and now the real person is declaring his feelings for you! It's like being in every romantic movie you ever watched. The key here may be to slow things down as you pray and see what happens when you do share your faith with him," Piper says.

"You could be the person to share the good news of Jesus with him when no one possibly has or in a way he would listen. I would be incredibly careful about letting your mind and heart go forward into the future until you really know if he is a man who loves the Lord. You want to be with someone where you both have the Lord as number one," Sister Mary-Margaret says.

"Everything you say makes so much sense, and yes, it goes against the longings in my heart. Please pray for me, both of you. I need it!" I say.

"We will be praying for you, in fact, we could pray more extensively right now, but Sister Mary-Margaret and I have an appointment we can't break. She's speaking at a ladies' church group in a half hour, and we have to be heading that way. I'm sorry to cut you short!" Piper says.

"Oh, look at me! I didn't even ask if you guys had time! I'm so sorry," I say.

"No, your timing was perfect! We got to talk, and I hope we helped. We sure do love you, Alice, and we will be praying. Let's all keep talking and praying about this. You don't have to tackle this alone," Sister Mary-Margaret says.

"And we will be there tonight for your show, praying for that too, and thank you for the tickets! Are you going to be okay to perform with everything going on in your head and heart?" Piper asks.

"Yes. I feel strong because I know you are praying, and He is with me. I've felt so much love and strength since I knew that I wanted to follow Him. And He gave me such good advisors, right when I need you both. I am reading the Bible all I can. There's so much to learn! Thank you for showing me more verses," I say.

"And here, I wrote them down for you, so you can look them up and read around them too, so you get the context of what is being said," Sister Mary-Margaret says handing me a piece of paper.

"Okay, off you both go to your ladies' meeting. You probably won't see me before the performance, only while on stage, but I'll be seeing you right after. I can't wait!" I say.

After saying my goodbyes to these dear ladies and Freddy, plus a quick cuddle with Bijou and Labyrinth, the little bell tinkle sends me on my way.

Hmm. This leaves me a little extra time. If they didn't have to be somewhere, I know I would have gabbed to closer to showtime. I think I'll go down near the school area, have a seat on the grass, and just let God speak to me while I look at The Straits, the Mackinac Bridge, and the glorious sky of this day.

Here I go, wading back through the tourists to a quieter area I'm so happy I discovered on one of my wanderings. Yes, sneakers off and toes in the grass. That's calming. Huh … I hear guitar music. Oh cute, a couple of kids are plunked down too, playing a guitar and a ukulele. This is a nice soundtrack to my thoughts. Lord, please take over this whole situation with J.D. I know You love him far more than I ever could, but I don't want to make a wrong move here. Help me to be wise and strong because all I want to do is be with him every minute of the day! And Lord …

"Uh, we don't mean to intrude …," The teenagers playing the instruments are right beside me.

"Oh, no problem. Can I help you?" I ask.

"Aren't you Alice, who played in J.D.'s show?" the young lady asks.

"We had seats pretty far back, but we think you are her," the young man adds.

"What gave it away? This stunning eye patch?" I ask laughing.

Seeing me laugh, they laugh, too.

"I honestly didn't think a thing about that," the young lady says, "but could you tell us how long you've been playing? We've never seen someone who can play so many instruments. I mean, you hopped from one to the other and made it look easy. We know it's not easy, and wow, did you ever astound us with your musical talent. I'm Gail by the way, and this is my friend Mike. We go to school here on the island and live here," Gail says.

"Glad to meet you, Gail and Mike," I say. "How fortunate are you to be here on the island! Do you ever get used to all the beauty?"

"Ha, well, it's all we've ever known, so we dream of other places, too. You know, places with a bigger music scene," Mike says. "How did you get to be a professional musician?"

"I actually grew up mostly in Cheboygan, working in my uncle's music store. It was the only one in the town, so maybe you've been there?" I ask.

"Yes, a couple of times, and now that you mention it, maybe I did see you! I was so enamored with the instruments; I didn't pay much attention to anything else. So, you left there and joined a band?" Gail asks.

"No … I wish! It just worked out for my uncle to close the store and loan me out for this gig at the Grand with J.D. All those long nights in the music store, I taught myself all of J.D.'s music on a variety of instruments. I had nothing else going on, so I practiced a lot. Not normal, right?" I ask laughing.

They both laugh and give me a look of expectation, like they want me to keep talking.

"So, here I am! I can't quite believe it myself. Who do you guys like to listen to, besides J.D.?" I ask.

"Oh man, so many!" Gail says. "Let's see, James Taylor,

Carly Simon, Paul Simon, all the Simon and Garfunkel stuff, Bread, Stevie Wonder …"

"Aretha Franklin, Linda Ronstadt, Doobie Brothers, The Beatles, Gladys Knight …" Mike continues.

"So, basically, you like everyone!" I say.

"Yes, pretty much. And I really like Amy Grant right now, too." Gail says.

"Amy Grant? I don't think I've heard of her," I say.

"Oh, she's a Christian artist, and really good. I love her music," Gail says.

"Christian artist?" I ask.

"Yes, you know, her songs help build people's faith in God, but not like in an old-style, hymn way," Mike says.

"That sounds right up my alley. I'll have to check her out," I say. "I recently started a new walk of faith, and I can use all the help I can get," I say, wondering how they will react.

"Cool!" Mike says. "We both go to a youth group at a church here on the island. We love studying the Bible."

"You're way ahead of me. I'm just getting started," I say.

"It's the best decision you could ever make, to follow Jesus," Gail says. "I really wish you were here longer, and you could give a couple of locals like us some guitar and music lessons," Gail says. "We goof around like you probably heard, but it's slow going."

"Practice and not giving up will get you far. Just keep working at it. I'm sorry to have to cut this short, but I do have a show tonight, so I better get back to the hotel. It was great to meet you, Gail and Mike, and I hope I run into you again. I'll pop down in the area another day if I can, and maybe you'll be practicing. Then I could see if I could give you a few tips," I say.

"That would be so cool," Mike says.

"We would love that, yes please," Gail says.

"Bye guys. Off I go," I say.

That was a pleasant encounter, Lord. Teens who love You, and now I know a Christian music artist to look into. I'll have to remember to ask Piper if she has some Christian music to recommend. I didn't realize there was much of that. I'd love to get some. Working my way back up the small hill by the school to the sidewalk leading up to the Grand, I can't believe how calm I feel with everything going on. I just know the Lord is going to see me through, and if I keep my focus on Him, things will work out. I know He will be with me and ...

"Alice!"

Off in my own world again, and I didn't see this unwelcome torpedo coming my way.

"Alice, glad I caught you. You'll be happy to know your services may be greatly diminished in the next day or so as the guys are doing much better. I'm sure you'll understand if you are relegated back to strictly a tech. I mean, that is what you were hired for," Montague says with a self-satisfied grin. The Grinch! That's what his grin reminds me of.

"I'm happy to hear they are doing better, and I'll do whatever J.D. wants. Afterall, he is the musical lead, not you," I say.

"Oh, I'm well aware of his position. Seems you have never been well aware of yours. Just don't be surprised if your perfect evening doesn't go exactly as you planned. And don't say I didn't warn you," he says, brushing past me and continuing down the sidewalk.

Glad he's getting far from me. The less I have to see him, the better. What did his comment mean? I don't know what this evening holds, but I guess I'm about to find out.

CHAPTER TWENTY-SIX

It sounds like a really large crowd tonight. Hearing their buzz as they chatter is making me a little nervous, but I want to stay focused on delivering a stellar show. It may be J.D. and my last night playing as a duo, and I want it to be perfect. Every note I play has to be flawless. I can't stand it; I have to go on stage and take one peek out of the curtain. Let's see … oh, good! Right in the front on the right side — Piper, Cam, Sister Mary-Margaret, and Freddy. Ah, Freddy looks so cute in his freshly pressed, dress-up shirt. He's beaming. I wish I could have had more time with both Cam and Piper together while I've been here but look at them. They are such a darling couple. And who is on the left in the front. Oh joy. Katherine Sims-Dubois and Vivian. Probably planning something and not something good for me. What's on her skirt tonight? Guitars! Seriously? Yes! The woman has guitars and musical notes on her skirt, musical notes around her collar, and big treble clefs on the toes of each shoe! This is the first non-Mackinac outfit I think I've ever seen her wear. Unbelievable!

"No peeking, lady," J.D. says coming up behind me and whispering in my ear.

"You scared me, and I'm already scared!" I say, giving him a tap on his arm as I close the curtain slit so no one can see in.

"Hey, that's my playing arm. Careful, I'm a big star, you know!" he says with a hearty laugh. "All set for a great night? I can't wait. And here's good news — the guys are doing much better," he says.

"That is good news, just what we were hoping for," I say.

"Yeah, they should be back in a few days. Since we don't have a show tomorrow night, this may be our last duet-type performance, unless of course I can talk you into making this a regular thing," he says.

"Quit teasing me. Seriously, I'm going to cherish tonight, these next moments. That's about all my brain can handle," I say. "Any last-minute changes or anything I should know about?"

"I'm not teasing. I'm serious. We will be talking more about this, young lady," he says, squeezing my hand. "As far as tonight, it's business as usual. I'm not expecting anything out-of-the-ordinary, except of course, I would never put you in the ordinary category. You are fantastic," he says with a kiss on my cheek. "Ready, my beautiful lady? It's showtime!"

I hear the announcement that it's a special acoustic show as we get settled on our stools and then the curtain slowly opens. With the spotlight, I can't see the crowd anymore. I'm thankful. I can focus on just J.D. and the music. We do create beautiful music, and it's a night I'll remember forever.

When we get to his signature song, he hits one note on his guitar, and the crowd knows what is coming. They rise to their feet and applaud so loudly; we wait until it dies down. Then, he starts the first few notes, and they go crazy again. As we work through the song, I know he'll do what he loves to do. We will drop out, and the crowd will do the lyrics while we accompany them and soak in the moment. After the verse, we jump back in for the final chorus. When we hit the last notes of "Raincheck," they erupt in cheering and clapping again, showing their appreciation for this magnificent musician and songwriter. I have to wipe the tears away, it's all so breathtaking.

Grabbing my hand, J.D. pulls me toward the front to take a final bow. I wish he would bow alone, but I can tell by the pull, I'm coming along. As we are bowing, he tells the crowd he has never met a musician like me, and he wants me to take a bow of my own. Ahh, I wish this wasn't happening, but I step out and take a little bow. The crowd is appreciative, and I gesture back to him. Afterall, he is the real musician. The crowd applauds again. We step back, and the curtain closes as I hear the people filing out. I'm glad I asked my friends to hang back, because I want to go out front with most of the people gone and give them all a hug. Turning to J.D., I'm mesmerized by the look on his face. It matches what is happening in my heart. I am hopelessly, madly in love with this man.

"You are amazing. Actually, that's not an adequate word. There isn't a word that describes what you did tonight. It's like you're in my head. I have never loved playing with anyone more, and that includes 'the greats' I've been with for different projects. They don't hold a candle to you. Thank you for stepping up these past few days. I know it won't be exactly the same when the guys come back, but I have loved these performances more than anything I've ever done. I mean that from the bottom of my heart," he says, pulling me closer.

"J.D., I love making true music with you. These last few nights have been everything to me. Thank you for letting me have this chance to play and sing with you. As long as I live, I will never forget it. Thank you from the bottom of *my* heart," I say not resisting.

He pulls me even closer and kisses me like he hasn't before. I think my heart and mind will explode all at the same time. I don't want to pull away, but I can hear people will be entering through the room any minute, and I don't want to cause a scene.

"I better get out there," I say. "Piper, Cam, and everyone is waiting, and I promised to say hello."

"Oh awesome. I thought that was them in the front, but you know how hard it is to see," he says. "I'll come with you. I'd love to say hello, too."

Making our way out to the front of the stage, J.D. waves to some lingering fans looking for autographs. He gives his usual head signal to Montague to handle them, so he doesn't get mobbed. Staying close to me, we move toward my group.

"Alice! Alice! What a night of music! You were spectacular! Give me a hug. You were just wonderful!" Piper says hugging me.

"Alice, really, first class. Simply amazing," Cam says with a pat on my shoulder.

"Miss Alice! I had to make myself sit still and not stand up and do a jig! That was the best concert ever!" Freddy said.

Taking my hand, Sister Mary-Margaret has tears in her eyes. "What a gift you have been given, and I am so excited about how you will use it. Bravo, my girl. Absolutely stunning," she says.

"Oh, and J.D., you were amazing too, of course! Didn't meant to slight you!" Piper says.

"Hey, let's give credit where it is due. Alice was the shining star, no doubt. It's great to see you all again," he says.

"Oh, I'm sorry, J.D.," Piper says turning to Cam. "This is my husband, Cam. You've met Freddy. And, this is our very dear friend, Sister Mary-Margaret."

"Great to meet all of you! Alice talks about you all, all the time, telling me what wonderful friends you have been. That's something really special," he says, shaking Cam's hand.

"J.D., uh, do you have a minute?" It's Montague tapping him on the shoulder.

"Sure, Monty, but just have the people wait one more minute. I'll be right with them for an autograph," he says, turning away from Montague and back to all of us.

"Uh, J.D., I took care of them, but this can't wait. It's the police!" Montague says.

All our heads turn toward the back of the room to see an officer coming our way.

"I'm looking for Alice Merveille. Is that you Miss?" The officer is looking right at me. "I was told you wear an eye patch, so I'm assuming you are Alice," he says.

"Yes, I'm Alice Merveille. What's the problem officer?"

"I have some questions, and I need you to come with me," the other officer says. Questioning by the police? What did I do?

"Hold up here, officer. What is she being accused of?" J.D. asks, looking as confused as I feel.

"J.D., I tried to get a hold of you, but then felt I should go to the police," a man approaching our group says.

"Doctor Blaine, what is happening?" J.D. asks.

"We got the tests back, and it turns out, all the guys were poisoned. It was a mixture of arsenic, strychnine, and cyanide," he says.

"Just like in the movie *Arsenic and Old Lace!*" Piper says. "Oops, sorry."

"Doctor Blaine, is it? What does that have to do with me?" I ask.

"I had three people point the finger at you. Two contacted me to let me know they had something suspicious to report about the band member's sickness and that they felt you were involved," Dr. Blaine says.

"Who came forward?" I ask.

"First, it was Montague Cheshire. He said you were acting suspiciously ever since the sickness, and I should ask around about you. That led me to Vivian Meyer who confirmed that she saw you messing with the snack cart that only the band had access to. She told me to contact Miranda Colter, who handles the snack bar," he said, turning and nodding to Miranda who has mysteriously appeared to stand next to Vivian and Montague.

"Have you all lost your minds? Alice would never have anything to do with any of this. These are all accusations and nothing more from people who think they run the show around here," J.D. says, glaring at the three.

"You are blind to what has been going on here, J.D. It's coming to light, and it's about time," Montague says.

"Yes, even if you think she's so great, your opinion of her will change now that you know what she's really like. She fooled you, but she didn't fool any of us. We have your best interest in mind, and we weren't going to stand by and let any of this happen," Vivian shouts.

"I asked her if she drank tea. She said no, she was allergic to it. That made it easy for her to poison the tea. She didn't have to trifle with the food. As the days rolled by, she could see the guys loved having some flavorful teas to choose from, not just soda in cans. She also knows J.D. sticks to water when he's on tour. She wouldn't have wanted to poison him, just the guys," Miranda says.

"All so she could do a solo show with you, J.D. And it worked, she pulled it off," Montague says, looking at me with searing eyes. "She didn't want to kill the guys mind you, just enough to make them really sick. All so she could get close to you and ..."

"And try to seduce you," Vivian finished.

"You're all crazy," J.D. says. "Listen, Alice, I'm going to get you a lawyer. Don't say anything to anyone. These three stooges aren't going to get away with this," J.D. says.

"I'm not understanding any of this! From the moment I got here and found my personal guitar smashed, until this moment, I don't know what you all have against me!" I say.

"Your personal guitar was smashed? I hadn't heard about

that," J.D. says. "Who do you think did that? Now that sounds really suspicious," he says.

"That was just to …" Miranda starts to say.

"Shut up! Just shut up, Miranda!" Vivian yells.

"Miranda, what do you know about Alice's guitar getting destroyed?" J.D. asks.

"I shouldn't have done it, but she paid me a ton of money, and my sister is sick. I needed the money," Miranda says, starting to cry.

"Vivian! You paid Miranda to smash Alice's guitar?" J.D. asks.

"No! *I* didn't *give* her the money … I …" Vivian says.

"I don't like the way you said 'I' and 'give.' You are hiding something," J.D. says.

"A smashed guitar is hardly something compared to poisoning people," Montague says.

"Oh really, Monty? Officer, it's sounding like Montague, Vivian, and Miranda are the people you should be questioning," J.D. says.

"From what Miranda said, you were always the last person to be near the snack cart, Alice. That's why it seems like you had the most opportunity to poison the tea," Dr. Blaine says.

"I didn't poison anything, I swear. I only smashed the guitar for the money!" Miranda says sobbing. "The money came with a note, so I did it. I needed the money." She continues to sob. "I knew it was wrong, but my sister … I needed the money for my sick sister!"

"So, Vivian, you didn't 'give' her the money, but you saw to it the money made the way to her. You did it ,Vivian, admit it," J.D. says.

"Fine! I did arrange for the money to be dropped off to her. I know what you're like when you get around a feeble female. You think you have to take care of them. And she's the epitome of pathetic, so you were sure to get all sentimental around her. I was sending a message that she better watch her back. Big deal.

Guitars are a dime a dozen. I'm sure she can get another one," Vivian says.

"It was very dear to me, and it can't be replaced," I say quietly. Piper and Sister Mary-Margaret each come on either side of me. I need their comfort right now.

"Listen, folks, a smashed guitar is certainly not a good thing, but that guy is right. It's nothing compared to trying to kill people with poison. I think you all better come in for questioning," the officer says.

"She asked what you drank, what the guys drank …" Miranda blurts out through sobs.

"She, who, Miranda? Was it Vivian?" J.D. asks.

"I couldn't care less what people drink. What are you talking about, Miranda?" Vivian yells.

"This is getting out of hand. Like I said, I think you should all come with me," the officer says, gesturing for us to follow him.

"That probably won't be necessary." A deep voice resonates from the shadows in the back of the room. We all turn at once to see Joe, the custodian walking toward us.

"Nope, you are all going down the wrong rabbit hole when it comes to who poisoned that tea that got the band sick. It didn't happen by anyone in this room," he says.

"Then who did it?" J.D. asks.

"I didn't think much of some things I saw until I heard your stories. Now it's clear who poisoned the tea," says Joe.

CHAPTER TWENTY-EIGHT

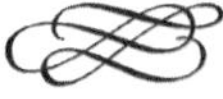

"And who are you?" the officer asks.

"I'm Joe, a custodian here at the Grand. You're newer, aren't you? I used to know the older guys on the force."

"Yes, I'm new, but I still want to know what you saw," the officer says.

"No problem, officer. I saw someone putting something in the tea after Miranda placed the cart in the green room. Alice was in the side music room. She didn't have anything to do with it. I know how to hang out in the shadows around here, so that lady didn't see me, but I saw her. She's the one who did it," Joe says.

"She, who? Who is she?" J.D. asks, glaring at Vivian and Miranda.

"I remember her name from that introduction meeting you had when you all first got here. Sally, I think she said," Joe says. "Something about being with the label, or on loan from the label. I remember her saying she was a Michigan girl. I was keeping an eye on everything when I saw her popping in and out of the room, looking around to see if anyone saw her, at least that's what it seemed like to me. I noticed because I haven't seen her around much, and honestly, I thought maybe she would want to have coffee with me. She stood in front of the cart for a while and kept looking around, so I held back where she couldn't see me to see what she was up to. It looked suspicious. I saw her take a packet out of her pocket and put it in the tea carafes, and then, she had a spoon in her other pocket and stirred it. All I could think was, to each their own. Maybe some kind of stuff to give the band a buzz, none of my business. I didn't think about it much until I heard your stories tonight. Now I can say without a doubt, she was poisoning that tea. I bet if you ask all those guys if they had tea that night, they will say yes. And J.D. and Alice, you didn't have any. There's your answer," Joe says.

"Where is this Sally … ?" the officer asks.

"Sally Wagner is her name. She's in charge of tickets and payroll on this tour, and yes, she's from Michigan and works for my record label. I had breakfast with her just this morning, and she said she had to leave the island for some business and would be in touch. Chances are, she's off the island already. She's the one you want to find," J.D. says. "I'll give you every number I have and, of course, the label executive numbers."

"What would be her motive?" the officer asks.

"She's been frantic this whole tour about numbers on the charts between me and this up-and-coming artist who is about to take over my spot. I could be wrong but piecing this together from the meetings I've been in, I think she stood to gain a huge promotion if this other artist moved to number one with his new song and his summer gig. Now it's apparent she desperately wanted that to happen for her own selfish reasons. There have been some very strange conversations in our meetings, which in the light of this, are making more sense. She might have thought she could wreck my numbers if I didn't have a band and I would have to cancel. But she hadn't counted on Alice. She's the one who saved the day, not the one who committed a crime," J.D. says, moving over behind me and putting his hands on my shoulders.

"Yes, it was her! She was the one who gave me money to find out what people liked to drink. But, after I asked around and got her the information she wanted, I felt bad about causing trouble for any of you. So, I didn't tell her the truth. Instead, I told her everyone drank tea. I didn't know what she was up to, but I figured it was no good. I still needed her money. You have to understand, my sister is sick and needs an operation. I'm sorry. I'm really sorry," Miranda says between bursts of sobbing.

"And I'm sorry everyone. It looks like I was way off base," Dr. Blaine says.

"It's okay, Doc. You couldn't have known," J.D. says.

"Let's not have anyone leave the island without checking with us. I'm sure I'll have more questions for all of you. In the meantime, I'll get an APB out on this Sally Wagner, and at least get her in for questioning to see what she has to say," the officer says. "Joe and Dr. Blaine, would you mind coming with me so I can take your statements? I'll start with you two, and I will be catching up with all of you. As I said, no one leave the island without talking to us first. All ticket options, boat operators, and airlines will be notified, so no funny business, please."

Everyone murmurs and nods in agreement.

"Absolutely, Officer. I have the final test results to give you," Dr. Blaine says.

"No problem, Officer. I'm glad to tell you everything. I don't want to see the wrong person get pinned for a crime. Alice didn't do it, and I wasn't going to let that happen on my watch," Joe says with a nod to me. "I felt bad I wasn't able to stop her guitar from being smashed. At least I could stop this false accusation."

Watching them walk away, I feel like I'm going to faint.

"Uh, Alice, sorry, I guess I was out of line," Montague says while keeping his eyes on J.D.

"Not now, Monty. We'll talk later. Meanwhile, can you go check on the guys and make sure they have everything they need," J.D. asks.

"Whatever you say, J.D.," Montague says, slinking away like a dog with his tail between his legs.

"Looks like Vivian has already snuck out. Miranda, I'll deal with you later," J.D. says.

"I'm so sorry, J.D., so sorry," she says dropping her head and leaving the room.

"Right now, Alice, and dear friends of Alice, what can I do for all you great folks? I'm so sorry you had to experience all that. My word. Such a great concert and such a disaster afterward! Really, my apologies to each of you and especially you, Alice," J.D. says putting his arm around me.

"I'm sure everyone is exhausted, but I'm sensing we need to just be together and chill a little bit. Why doesn't everyone come over to our cottage, and I'll throw some pizzas in the oven. How does that sound to everyone?" Cam asks.

"Yes, please come to our place. We'll all decompress. What do you think J.D. and Alice?" Piper adds.

"J.D., that actually sounds pretty calming to me. What about you?" I ask.

"Yes, exactly what we need. Is it close?" J.D. asks.

"It's right off the end of the porch here at the Grand. I'll show you," I say.

"How about you Freddy and Sister Mary-Margaret? How about a little pizza?" Cam asks.

"Sounds good to me, Mr. Cam," Freddy says.

"Yes, sounds wonderful," Sister Mary-Margaret agrees.

"I want to stop up in my room and change, and J.D., you probably want to do the same, so we'll meet you at your place in about a half hour," I say.

"Perfect. I'll have the pizza close to ready when you come," Cam says.

"Wait until you taste his pizza. It's so delicious," I say to J.D. trying to regain some sense of calm.

"I'll change quick and wait for you on the porch, Alice." J.D. says.

"Perfect. I won't take long. I'll see you all soon," I say heading for my room.

I need a minute. After closing my door, the tears come. It feels like a rush of tension escaping with each splash down my cheek. *Deep breaths, Alice.*

Dear Lord, thank You for saving me from going through the steps of being accused of a crime! Lord thank You for having Joe at the right place at the right time. I know You saved me, again!

Okay. Pull it together, Alice. A splash of chilly water, a make-up touch-up, jeans, and a casual shirt. I'm going to spend the evening with the people I love. Now, if one of them could learn about the greatest love of all time. If only.

It was a good decision to be together. Cam's pizza and the sweet companionship of all of them was exactly what I needed. I could tell J.D. enjoyed them as much as I do. He was super interested in Sister Mary-Margaret's life. I liked learning more about her too, her family, and how she became a nun. J.D. was blown away by the work she is doing in Africa and wanted to know how he can donate to her cause. She promised to let him know.

I guess it was dumb to think we would all get into a deep conversation about Jesus, and J.D. would give his life to God. I would have loved that, but Cam and Piper know how to read people. Not everyone arrives on Piper's doorstep as raw and broken as I was when I met her. I was also thinking it would be so easy for them to tell him everything and then it wouldn't be left up to me. I feel like a chicken. Lord, I know You will help me say what I need to say when the time is right. The time flew by. None of us were ready to part, but everyone seemed to sense the time was right.

Holding hands as we walk back to the Grand after this calming aftermath, J.D. pulls on my hand while I'm turning toward the direction of the rooms.

"Stay with me a little longer," he says. "Let's go to the music room."

"Really? You don't think we'll get in trouble or something this late? Aren't you tired?" I ask.

"I want more time alone with you. It's secluded. No one will even know we're there," he says pulling me again in the direction of the Grand Hall. "I have set something up for you."

I don't know what this is, but my pulse is racing. It is noticeably quiet as we enter the hall and then the music room.

"I'll get the lights," I say starting to reach behind the door.

"No, don't. Hang on. Let me light these candles I put here just for this moment," he says.

Moving around the room, he lights several candles, each one adding shadows and flickers to this precious place where we've shared so much together.

"There ... doesn't that look lovely? Just enough light to not spoil the moment," he says. "Okay, now, you sit over here on this stool, and I'm going across the room for your surprise."

What in the world is happening? He's picking up his guitar, getting it settled on his lap, and staring intently at me.

"This is a song I've been working on. It's only an instrumental so far because I want the words to be perfect. I'm not there yet. But I want you to hear the music anyway. It's a piece I'm calling, 'Alice.'

My heart feels like it's going to leap out of my body! As his fingers move deftly over the frets in an enchanting melody that blends his signature style with some new things I've never heard from him before, I have to remember to breathe. Landing on the last note, he hits the final chord and puts the guitar down. I can't even speak!

"Alice. Come here," he says.

"J.D., that was the most beautiful melody I've ever heard and ..."

"Come here. Come next to me," he says.

"J.D. Honestly, with the way I'm feeling right now ... I'm

not sure that is such a good idea. I mean, we are here alone, and my heart is bursting right now …"

"Come here," he says softly yet more commanding this time.

I can't help myself. As I move closer to him, he pulls me the last few steps. With him on the stool, we are face to face.

"Alice, it's very dim in here, and we are alone. I want to take off the patch, and I want to kiss your face. Not just the one side. I want to kiss your whole face," he says gently.

"You don't want to do that really. I, it's bad. I …"

"Let me take the patch off and let me kiss you the way I want to kiss you," he says.

All I can do is nod as he removes the patch. I'm standing in front of him with my whole face showing, in front of the first person who has seen me without it. His soft kisses move around my cheek, my eye, and down the side of my face that I have spent so many years hiding.

"Never, ever, be sad about this face again. Do you promise me? It's the most beautiful face in the world, and you need to know that," he whispers in my ear.

Putting the patch back on gently he pulls me closer again.

"And now, you need sleep, my beauty. So, I'm going to walk you back to your room and then head to mine, because this has been one heck of a day, to say the least."

That has to be the understatement of the century.

CHAPTER TWENTY-NINE

Oh, the man can kiss. I'm still lingering in those feelings even though we had to be apart for these hours. Is today the day I talk to J.D. about You, Lord? Lying in bed here with the sun once again welcoming me to a new day, I'm fortunate to have slept at all after such an evening. Before we parted last night after that sweet time in the music room, J.D. let me know he has rented a carriage for us today. He will be the driver and promised we can go wherever we want to go on the island. With only one more week of concerts, I have no idea what the future means for me —

for us. I know what Piper and Sister Mary-Margaret told me is true. I know it. But the way I feel for him, it's all consuming!

Lord, help me do what You want me to do. Show me what to do.

And once again I jump when the phone rings! J.D. and I are all set on a time, so not sure who this could be. Maybe Piper checking on me?

"Hello? Yes, this is she. Oh, yes, I had a wonderful time meeting them. Uh huh. Uh huh. So, you would need …. Oh, wow. That's something I've never thought about here, but I do have experience. Oh, you saw the concert,

too? Well, let me think about it, and can I get back to you? Yes, I can reach you there. Yes, yes, I will. Thank you for thinking of me. Bye."

Well, that was a phone call I did not see coming. Hmm … a lot to think and pray about, but right now I have to rush, or I'll be late for my ride with J.D. Come hungry he'd said, there will be a breakfast picnic on our adventure.

"Don't you love the *clip-clop, clip-clop* you hear all the time on the island? I love horses," J.D. says as we round a corner on a road in our own private carriage. "I think I'd like to own some, someday,"

"I had no idea you were a horse *and* a tandem bike aficionado. Do your talents know no bounds?" I say, giving him a smile, I hope he sees as filled with love.

"How are you doing? Did you sleep last night?" J.D. asks.

"Yes, surprisingly, I did okay. I was full of pizza and quite relieved not to be spending the night in jail," I say.

"I'll be anxious to hear if they caught up with Sally. I'm not sure what she will get charged with, but I hope they throw the book at her. She has been acting so weird since she got to the island. I should have paid more attention and realized there was something off by how she was acting," he says.

"Well, I think it's reasonable to expect that someone you work with isn't crazy, present company excluded of course," I say.

"Of course." I love his smile so much.

"I was flabbergasted last night by Miranda! Vivian, well, par for the course. But I thought Miranda was more trustworthy. I've worked with her off and on over the past few years. Thank goodness she decided not to tell Sally the truth. I'm sorry the guys got sick, but it could have been all of us. All because Sally wanted a higher position with the label. What a crazy move," he says.

"Sally sure covered up her deception well. I do feel bad for Miranda. I'm not saying what she did was right, but she seems desperate to help her sister," I say.

"If she would have come to me, I would have helped her. As it is, I've tasked Monty with finding out how I can help financially. And, we are arranging for Miranda to get some counseling," he says.

"That is so nice of you. Hopefully, she can get it all solved," I say.

"Milady, enough about that. Let's pull over here. I have a piping hot thermos of coffee, and a sweet breakfast spread made by the Grand chef for our breakfast. Sound good?" he asks.

"Perfect as always when you are in charge," I say.

Pulling over, we get settled on a nice blanket on the grass. It's lovely to be in this more remote part of the island where there aren't a lot of tourists out and about this early. The occasional biker or two go by, but they are busy with their destination and don't seem to pay much attention to us.

"So, Alice, why didn't you tell me about the guitar? It was one you had most of your life, wasn't it? I wish you would have told me," he says.

"I didn't know you, and I didn't want to make a big deal with my new employer. I got off on the wrong foot with Montague and thought maybe he had done it. I even asked him, but he denied it, and I believed him. I thought it was best to let it go," I say. "If I knew you, like I know you now, I would have said something."

"That's good to know. You realize our time here is almost over. The next week will be non-stop shows, and then the gig is up. What a ride! At least I don't have to worry about officially breaking up with Vivian. As I understand it, she's already checked out of the Grand and is on her way to Europe. She didn't even say good-bye, which I'm perfectly okay with. It does speak to her character — what she's really like beyond the façade I've seen over the past few months," he says.

"She seemed like a very threatened person. I thought she wanted to be friends, but really, she was playing me. I guess I am naive that way, but I'm trying to wise up. She set me up pretty good," I say.

"Anyway, let's not talk about any of them. Let's talk about us. What would you think about staying on tour with me? It's not a tour like we are doing shows now. It's more of a publicity tour, but you could come along with me. I'll be in lots of cities, so you'll see cool cities across America. Wouldn't that be fun?" he asks.

"We wouldn't be playing and singing?" I ask.

"No, it's a lot of interviews for me, some song writing. But lots of free time. We could hang out a lot," he says.

"So, you're asking me to not come as a musician but as your girlfriend?" I ask.

"Yes, that's the way to put it. My girlfriend. I love the sound of that. It's a bit of a party lifestyle, you know, typical rock guy stuff. Definitely not the tranquil life we've been living here on the island. I've loved it, but it's not what I'm used to. I'm ready to get back to my regular life a bit. I am more of a big city guy when it comes down to it," he says.

See, Alice, there is something you didn't know about J.D. You would have thought he could live on the island forever if given the chance.

"I don't know. I think I could stay here on this island forever. It is feeling like home," I say.

"Ah, wherever you are feels like home. But you haven't seen the big cities yet. You might be surprised with what you will see, and you might like it. It has it's taxing moments when people get too crazy, chasing me in the car and things like that, but it's all part of what I signed up for," he says. "Anyway, think about it. You won't have to worry about accommodations or anything. Monty will set it all up," he says.

"You are sticking with Monty, huh?"

"Yeah, he will get a good tongue lashing, and then he will act correctly because he knows he's on a probation. He has done a decent job for me as a manager, but he really messed up when it came to you and this gig," he says.

"You do know he's a totally different person with you than anyone else, don't you?" I ask.

"Probably not as much as I should, but because of everything, yes, now I'm seeing it. And I will be talking to him about that. Don't be worried that he will give you a hassle because he won't. I promise," he says.

Oh, J.D., you loyal man. I don't think that leopard changed his spots as much as you think he did, but that's not my call.

"So, you'll think about coming with me?" he asks tenderly.

"I'll think about it. Even better, I'll pray about it," I say watching how he reacts.

"Pray? Sure, why not. Say a prayer to all the big hitters: Buddha, Jesus, Muhammed … hit them all up for advice," he says.

"No, for me, it's only praying in Jesus's name," I say. "He said He is The Way, The Truth, and the Life, and that no one comes to the Father except through Him because of how He died on the cross for our sins," I say.

Thank you, Holy Spirit. I should have known You would give me the right words at the right time.

"Hmm. I heard a lot about that when I was in California in something they had called the Jesus Movement in the early 70s. I talked to a few people about it, but it just doesn't add up for me. But you know, live, and let live. Everyone should go on their own path, I believe," he says.

"Have you ever read the whole book of John in the Bible?"

"No, can't say that I have. I mostly listened to other people and kind of knew it wasn't adding up."

"Would you read the book of John if I got you a modern version Bible?"

"Read the Bible? Well, I'm not terribly interested, but if you want me to, I would."

"With an open mind?"

"Yes, with an open mind if that would make you happy. And I'll also do it with one more stipulation. You have to let me give you a new guitar. I'll pick it out, and you have to accept it. Would you let me do that? Fair deal?"

"That is extremely generous of you, and yes, it's a deal," I say.

"Shake on it?"

"Kiss on it."

"Okay, sealed with a kiss," he says as I lean in, and he gently kisses me.

"Do you have something lined up? You said you are done with your uncle's music shop, right?"

"Yes, he's sold the shop and moved to Florida already. I have to remember to get all the instruments signed too, you know, for the auction house. If I don't, I'll have to deal with him again," I say.

"So, you are free to come with me …"

"Praying about it, remember?" I say with a wink.

"Yes, I remember. Well, shall we continue on this carriage ride, milady?"

"Yes, that sounds lovely."

A quick pick-up of this delicious feast, and we are on our way. We both know stopping at the main tourist sites is off-limits because of who he is but meandering on the back roads and stopping periodically to sit by the shore is still so satisfying. I love being with him, near him, and listening to his many stories of life on the road. It does sound exciting, and I haven't been to many cities. I wish I could follow my heart and freely tell him I'll follow him on the publicity tour, but there's a tug that tells me differently. I wasn't kidding. I really have to read my Bible and pray about this.

CHAPTER THIRTY

The rest of the shows are pure fun and music magic. Every show is filled, and the crowds are always so enthusiastic. The Grand has made this last week fan week, so J.D. is super busy signing autographs and posing for pictures. We sneak in a breakfast, and then he's off for the day. I miss seeing him. It's good to see the guys doing well with no lasting ramifications from the poisoning. All too soon, the shows are done.

The police catching Sally Wagner while she was trying to leave the country made the national news, and it was the major headline in the Mackinac Island newspaper. Time away from J.D. has given me the prayer time I wanted and time to visit with Piper and Sister Mary-Margaret. I know they are praying for me; I can feel it. J.D. has carved out one last evening for us before the last concerts. He gently keeps asking if I'm coming on his publicity tour, and I am trying to keep my answers vague for as long as I can. I don't know my answer yet. At least Montague has been more civil to me, but he's also pressing me. I get it. He has to make arrangements.

Everything is packed up and on its way to the auction house. Thank goodness Joe helped me with such an enormous task!

J.D. offered, but he was tied up again with label meetings after Sally's quick departure.

My music man said 'yes' to my note asking him if he would be willing to visit the Labyrinth below the Grand after dinner. I want him to see how beautiful it is. I assured him there is rarely anyone there, especially toward the evening. I'm still tickled I found a sparkling blue dress with forget-me-not's embroidered around the border of the neck. And darling little blue Swarovski earrings. It was a splurge, but it's so perfect.

Oh, God! That was You too — finding me a forget-me-not dress. You do care about the little things. I know the Labyrinth is the right time to give him my decision. Lord, do I have a future with J.D.?

Yes, the look on his face when we meet for dinner tells me my dress splurge was worth it.

Savoring every morsel of this last big dinner together at the Grand, there's a part of me that still can't believe this has all happened. I can't stop looking at him as we leave the dining hall, walk down the long stairs, across the lawn, around the pool area, and to the opening of the labyrinth.

"So, this is your special little spot that you love so much? It's really cool. Do you walk the path?" he asks.

"I do. I walk it and pray," I say. "I've spent some special reflection time in here. It feels sacred to me," I say.

"Yes, I can feel that," he says. "It's beautiful, like this gorgeous woman in the forget-me-not dress."

"J.D. ..."

"I know, Alice. I know you're not coming with me, and it's breaking my heart. I don't want to be away from you."

"Oh, no. No broken hearts, please," I say, squeezing his hand as we sit down on the bench next to the Labyrinth path. "You're right. I'm not coming with you. I'm not saying I'll never do music with you again, but I'm not coming with you on this trip, this time. I've found a foundation here with Piper and Sister Mary-Margaret, and I'm not ready to leave it yet. They are so strong in their faith, and I need to learn from them," I say.

I'm watching his eyes, but he isn't saying anything, just watching me and squeezing my hand.

"And I was offered the opportunity to teach a music class and private music lessons to the students at the school here this fall. I didn't ask for this opportunity. The school principal called me after I met some kids at the school park when I was sitting in the grass one afternoon. They approached him about me teaching. That phone call helped make it clear to me — that's what I'm supposed to do," I say. "Piper and Cam have offered that I can stay with them while they help me get a place here. So, I have a job and a place to stay with people who have become important to me. You are extremely important, too. In fact, I can say I love you so much. But we have vastly different lives, and it's going to take time to know each other better."

"So basically, God is going to keep you from me? That's not a checkmark in His favor!" he says with a wink, but I also see a tear rolling down his cheek. "You know, I'm not used to not getting the girl, but then I'm not usually competing with God."

I love his sense of humor.

"I know this is hard. I think God is going to be showing me a whole lot of things that are important in life and helping me to become a whole person and heal from my past," I say, wiping away his tear. "And I think, if you'll read the book of John, and continue to read the Bible, there is a whole lot there for you, too. That's what I think."

"I mean, I'm spiritual. I can relate. But, for me, it's more nature. You know, appreciating the earth, the sky, the land. I've just never been a fan of religion," he says.

"A few months ago, I wasn't thinking about any of this either, so I get it. But it's not religion. It's a relationship with God through Jesus. And you also get to know the Holy Spirit — it's hard to understand until you truly believe. Piper showed me a verse that says something to the effect: what is in the Bible seems foolish to an unbeliever. But, for the believer, the truth opens up," I say.

"So, Piper, Cam, and even Freddy thinks this way, too? Obviously, Sister Mary-Margaret …"

"Yes. It was meeting Piper on the boat over here that led me to talk with me about God. She's the one who introduced me to seeing Jesus as your personal Savior. It's the verse from John 3:16. '*For God so loved the world that he gave his one and only Son, that whoever believes in him shall not perish but have eternal life.*' She told me to put my name in there. For God so loved Alice, for God so loved J.D …."

"God so loved J.D. …" he repeats softly.

"When that truth hit my heart, I had to know more for myself, on a much more personal level. And that's what I'm going to pray for you as you go onto your next thing," I say, leaning my head on his shoulder. "And, if we were ever to be together, I'd want you to have a whole, loving person in your life — not a person for the current moment. I would be in it for the long haul, but we have to be on the same page in our beliefs. It's that important to me," I say, watching his face for a reaction.

"You are unlike any girl I have been with, that is for sure. So smart, so beautiful, so unique, and so messing with my mind right now. Your name, Merveille — you truly are a wonder. That's the perfect name," he says as another tear escapes.

"Funny thing is, I didn't even know that's what my name meant until you told me. But now, I do love it more."

"My wonder lady, I don't know if I can live up to what you need. But I'm willing to do the next step. I will be reading the Bible, I will. Why the book of John?"

"Well, from what I can understand, the whole Bible is a big story — the story of God's unrelenting love to be with each of us and love us. It seems that John is a good place to get an overview of the life of Jesus and how God sent Him to reconnect with us after we turned away from Him. That's what Sister Mary-Margaret told me. Of course, you can read anything you want, but to hone it down, let's start with John. That's where I'm diving in right now, and then I'll move on to Luke. I already have a modern-day language Bible for you. It doesn't have the 'thees' and 'thous' that I think are hard to wade through."

"That does sound more promising. I didn't realize there were more modern versions. Yeah, I like the idea. It sounds more appealing. And then, I'll call you, and we can talk about what I'm learning. How about that?" he says.

"That would be something I would love. So, are you super disappointed?"

"I'm relieved that you don't want to call it quits and not see me ever again." He strokes my cheek. "Looks like I have to find out if I can get a raincheck on you," he says with a big smile.

"Okay, good one. And not see you again? Quite the opposite. I could run off with you and let what happens, happens. But, I know, that isn't what is right for me, and I don't believe it's right for you either."

"I will be thinking about you, a lot, and this time we've had together on this magical island. I have a feeling I'm going to be writing a lot of love songs for my next album. And, oh yeah, I almost forgot. Look at these," he says, reaching into his suit pocket and pulling out pictures from our bike ride to Arch Rock. "These are for you, so you don't forget me," he says, handing me five pictures.

"Oh, they turned out great! You have a knack for getting two people into one shot. I'll treasure these."

"You can't have this one," he says, showing me the shot of me in the forget-me-nots. "It's all mine. See. Your eyes are the exact color of the flowers, and the sun is perfect. This is going with me everywhere. You'll still be with me," he says.

Oh, this man. He sees me as having eyes and doesn't see the patch. How I'm going to miss him! Now, there's a tear falling down my cheek. He wipes it away and replaces it with a kiss.

"Look! There's a full moon, just for us tonight!" he says, holding me close.

"Think of it. Wherever you are, and wherever I am, we will still be under that same moon," I say.

"Yes, it will always be *our* Mackinac moon. I love you, Alice, and I'm willing to wait until we can be under this same moon again, sometime in the future," he says, giving me another hug.

"Yes, J.D. It's *our* Mackinac moon forever."

Taking in the fresh Straits' air and looking at the stars over the Grand Hotel joining in the glow of the moon on the rocks in the labyrinth, I'm at peace. I don't know what the future holds, but I finally know the One who holds the future. And it will be filled with goodness.

The End

I Peter 1:8 NIV

Though you have not seen him, you love him; and even though you do not see him now, you believe in him and are filled with an inexpressible and glorious joy.

Luke 9: 23-24 NIV

Then he said to them all: Whoever wants to be my disciple must deny themselves and take up their cross daily and follow me. For whoever wants to save their life will lose it, but whoever loses their life for me will save it.

Isaiah 43:19 NIV

See, I am doing a new thing!
Now it springs up; do you not perceive it?
I am making a way in the wilderness
and streams in the wasteland.

A special thank you to my singer-songwriter son, Benjamin Olson of Nashville.

A special thank you to my son Benjamin for allowing me to use his lyrics and finished song for the fictional character of J.D. in this novel. It's another unique experience with a novel from Lake Girl Publishing!

Hear "Raincheck" on iTunes here: https://music.apple.com/us/album/rain-check-single/1578185525

and

You Tube here: https://bit.ly/3iIP3RG

Download music from Benjamin Olson from your favorite music site like Apple, Google, and Spotify.

"Rain Check"© Benjamin Olson.

For any music inquiries, email me at info@lakegirlpublishing.com

Dear Reader,

I hope you got lost in the beauty of Mackinac Island and the truth of the story of Alice Merveille. If you've never been to Mackinac Island, it's glorious. If you have been to the island, or perhaps this was your read on a vacation — you will feel like you are on another virtual visit in another time. My husband and I have visited Mackinac Island for over thirty years, and the magic is always there.

Alice was challenged about her faith and the abundant life that awaits anyone who chooses Jesus as Savior. It's a free gift, available to all. There's a forever family that awaits each of us with a call to magnificent love. That's what life is all about!

What's up next? Another journey to magical Mackinac Island in 1982 with *Being Wendy (In a world afraid to grow up)*. Keep reading, because the first chapter is coming up!

Please stay in touch for the latest news and sometimes a giveaway!

Facebook.com/LakeGirlPublishing

My private Facebook team — Piper's Island Peeps:

Facebook.com/groups/piperpenn

Twitter @MoDawnWriter

Instagram.com/lakegirlpublishing

My email. (I love to hear from readers!) Info@LakeGirlPublishing

My website: LakeGirlPublishing.com

My heartfelt thanks,
Michèle

Ten Things You Can Do to Be a Part of my Piper Peep's Island Team!

1. **Leave a review**. If you liked the books, leave a kind review. Reviews can be short and sweet, but never give away plot lines or spoilers. Your encouraging words may be the catalyst that introduces someone else to the story — very important! From Goodreads to all the places books are sold online, your review matters.
2. **Talk about this book on your social media platforms.** Tell your friends that you enjoyed it. Go to other reader Facebook sites like Avid Readers of Christian Fiction and sites that love Mackinac Island and recommend my books.
3. **Ask your local library to carry the book(s).** In addition, *Being Ethel (In a world that loves Lucy)* is also available in an audiobook, often popular for library borrowing.
4. **Ask your local bookstore to bring the books in.** They will know how to order in from their usual sources — simply give them the titles.
5. **Contact me to speak at your women's group.** Does your women's group need a speaker? I am a speaker for women's groups as well as being an author.
6. **Let me know who you are through my website.** Sign up and get my newsletters.
7. **Use these books as gifts!** Email me if you'd like a sticker for the inside of the book, personalized to someone.
8. **Check out my non-fiction book: *5 Easy Steps to a Happy Birthday!*** No adult should ever have a ho-hum birthday ever again. You can have a Happy Birthday, on your terms. Whether your birthday is

soon or months away — now is the time to enact the five easy steps! Available everywhere for the price of a greeting card. It also makes a fabulous gift.

9. **Pray for me!** I appreciate your prayers! My books have a message of hope and faith, and my desire is to get them to as many people as possible.
10. **Interact with me on social media.** Follow my Facebook.com/LakeGirlPublishing page and my private team Facebook page, Piper's Island Peeps, for those who are very enthusiastic about my books:

www.LakeGirlPublishing.com/connect
Facebook.com/groups/piperpenn
Twitter @MoDawnWriter
Instagram.com/lakegirlpublishing
My email. (I love to hear from readers!) Info@LakeGirlPublishing
My website: LakeGirlPublishing.com

Thank you for being a part of my team:
Piper Penn's Island Peeps!

Meet Michèle Olson

Michèle Olson has an over forty-year career in advertising and marketing as a writer in all mediums, with an emphasis in health writing. She has also enjoyed a professional voice career including time as a DJ (yes, even when they still played records!) and continues to voice local to national commercials and voice projects.

It has always been her dream to segue into fiction and *Being Ethel (In a world that loves Lucy)* was her first in a series based on Mackinac Island — a tiny island in the Straits of Mackinac that connect the Upper and Lower Peninsula of Michigan. A visitor there, along with her husband, for over thirty years, she loves to tell people about this unique place with no cars and plenty of fudge! She is thrilled to keep the series going with *Being Dorothy (In a world longing for home)* and this new offering *Being Alice (In a world lost in the looking glass.)*

A mom, a mother-in-love, and a "Gee Gee" (G as in good), Michèle resides with her husband in the shadow of Lambeau Field, where life around football abounds. She cherishes her faith and family above all and is delighted to take you on another trip to Mackinac Island, a place that has brought her so much respite and joy.

She loves connecting, so reach back through all the social media links provided. Next? It's a trip back to Mackinac in *Being Wendy (In a world lost in the looking glass)*. It's book four in the series.

Ten places to explore if you go to Mackinac Island!

1. **Arch Rock.** This is a natural rock bridge that sits 149 feet above the Straits of Mackinac as if it's suspended in mid-air! You can walk there, or you can stop as part of a carriage tour. It's fun to see from below or up close.

2. **Fort Mackinac**. Known to be the oldest building in Michigan, you can see history come alive and imagine yourself living in a military outpost. It's the fortress on a bluff you see as you come into the harbor. Listen at certain times of the day — the cannon does work!

3. **St. Anne's Catholic Church.** This beautiful church is worth seeing, including the stain glass windows. Of course, if you're like me, you imagine Sister Mary-Margaret sitting in a pew just waiting to have a conversation with you.

4. ***Somewhere in Time,*** the wonderful movie filmed on the island in 1979 and part of *Being Ethel (In a world that loves Lucy),* my first novel in this series, boasts multiple island treasure stops. Seek out the "Is it you?" spot with a plaque commemorating the line and, of course, the famed gazebo. Relocated from its original place in the movie, anyone on the island can tell you where to find it!

5. **Fort Holmes**. Do you like to hike? Go to this highest point on the island, even higher up than Fort Mackinac. Originally named Fort George, it was renamed when the American returned to the fort in 1815. In 2015, it was reconstructed for visitors to learn more about its amazing history.

6. **Round Island Lighthouse.** You'll pass this beautiful lighthouse as you ferry in and away from the island. Not a spot for visitors, as much as

sightseers, you'll find yourself looking for it whenever you are near the shores of the island. It, too, has a pivotal scene in *Somewhere in Time*. Besides, don't you just love lighthouses?

7. **Eagle Point Cave.** Once again, it's for the hiker in you! Located on the north side of the island. When you are there, read about some of the tall tales surrounding this interesting spot.

8. **Sugar Loaf.** It's an adventurous hike or bike ride to make it to this tall geological formation but worth it. How many times have you seen a limestone stack on an island? You see my point!

9. **The Grand Hotel**. Of course! Either go for a stay or pay the minimal fee and walk around for a day. Be sure to sit on that famous porch on a white wicker rocking chair and imagine you are having a conversation with Piper Penn!

10. **The Island Bookstore.** Located inside The Lilac Tree entrance on Main St., this wonderful bookstore has been bringing the best in books to island visitors for decades! You can get a Mackinac Island favorite or browse the wide variety of books available. Stop in and take a picture of my books! **Send me a pic of you there with my book(s), and I'll send you a wonderful treat in the mail!**

This list could go on and on. Little Stone Church, The Butterfly House, Anne's Tablet, The Visitor's Center, the Biddle House, and all the historic sites, the fudge, the food, the fun! It's all beyond wonderful, and I hope every reader gets to have a visit someday! Until then, you can go there through my books anytime you want. I'll be looking for you!

BEING WENDY

(IN A WORLD AFRAID TO GROW UP)

Arriving in 2022

Enjoy this glimpse into the fourth book in the Mackinac Island
Story Series

Michèle Olson © 2021
 LakeGirlPublishing.com
 info@lakegirlpublishing.com

BEING WENDY

(IN A WORLD AFRAID TO GROW UP)

Early Spring 1982
"Happy Birthday to you …"

Look at all of them, their faces glowing in the reflection of my fifty birthday candles. All smiles. All trying to make it look like good-natured ribbing about age and every one of them a liar! Which one is the rat that is trying to end my career? None of them should know my secret, but all of them want to be living the life I'm living. Who is it? Who found out and wants to get me? Snitch!

All these years, I've tolerated the hints to the paparazzi. Each one of them taking their turn to tip off a photographer who tried to capture me in my unglamorous moments. Always, the goal to get me on a mag rag cover looking my worst. I've done it to a few of them, too. It's part of the game. But this is different. I've never done anything to make them lose their status or their livelihood. So, it has to be one of them.

"Happy Birthday to you …"

Every single one of them green with envy when I hit the bestseller list over and over again. And after I got engaged to the Baron — oh the acting! I thought some of them would faint from exhaustion at the displays of feigning happiness for me.

Fakes! They all deserve Academy Awards for their performances. They don't give a fig about my well-being.

"Happy Birthday, dear Wendy!"

Grow up, you blackmailers! Grow up, you cheats! You society ladder climbers who pretend to be my friends but stab me in the back any chance you get! You pathetic lost boys and girls, always clamoring to be kings and queens of the land, never caring who you walk over to reach the top.

"Happy Birthday to you!"

"Oh, you are all so dear to remember me on this momentous day. I mean, fifty is the new forty, right?" I say with the sweetest fake smile I can muster. The only one in this room I can trust is the Baron. Even he is leaving on a three-month business trip to Africa — leaving me alone with this crowd of vipers. He made it clear it wasn't prudent to bring me along. I don't know how I feel about that. And mousy-little Sylvia even showed up for my party. Her birthday wishes are probably the sincerest. She knows who signs her paychecks. At least she's a decent assistant. How does the girl even see out of those thick glasses? I really should give her some advice on how to dress.

"Make a wish!"

Of course, Muffy would be the first to yell that out. She's always on my heels, copying my every move. I wonder if the real world has any clue how competitive life is in our writing circle — the catty things that happen in the "Who's Who" of the LA in-crowd of authors and screenwriters.

"Yes, make a wish," they are all yelling now.

Sukie, Biff, Cromwell, Tito, Kat … They're all yelling and staring at me. Doesn't anyone in LA have a real name? And here I am, fifty, about to have my whole career ruined.

I wish there were somewhere I could escape and wait! That's it! Kat! Kat's name reminds me of … what was her name at the boarding school? She sends that over-the-top Christmas card every stinking year from that island where she lives. Katherine Sims-Dubois! That's it. Those big swirly letters when she signs the card. Good ole boarding school classmate, Katherine. Every single year, a card yammering on about that Midwest island. You'd think it's Martha's Vineyard or Catalina or something. I'm sure no one in this crowd or the paparazzi knows a thing about that little speck on the map she calls home.

What a perfect place to hide! I'll dig out her Christmas card and see where it is. Michigan island? No, that's not it. Doesn't matter. Her card will have the name. There's some hotel there with a big porch — I'll stay there. I'll use a different name. Yes, that will work. No one will know I'm there. I won't tell anyone, not even Baron. I won't even tell Katherine! If I bring all my wigs, she won't recognize me. I mean, come on, we've all aged in thirty years. I'll scope her out before I let her know I'm there. Who knows if I can trust even her?

"Make a wish! Make a wish!" they are all yelling.

I like this idea! Yes, I can make this happen! I can disappear into that island.

"Make a wish before the place burns down from all those candles," Moxie says. Ugh. These people. How clever they find themselves to be.

"Oh, don't worry. I'm making a big wish! One that I have no doubt will come true!" I say, sucking in a big gulp of air so I can blow with all my might. Then, moving around and over the cake, I do it! I catch every last candle and snuff it out. There, now, could you all just leave? Well, not Baron, of course. Oh, and Sylvia.

"I hope I was part of your wish, my love," Baron says, putting his arm around my shoulder.

"Oh, always, my sweet," I say.

What I won't say for prestige and money! Hey, there's only so many fish in the pond these days. It's no one's business why I choose to call him Baron instead of by his real name. Besides, the look on people's faces when they find out I'm engaged to British royalty is so delicious.

I've got it! I'll be Lily. Lily, what? Lily ... Darling! The perfect name to hide behind — Lily Darling. *Think Wendy.* How will you keep on top of things? Hmmm. I'll get a Post Office box on the island under my new name. Getting a few fake documents will be no trouble. Oh, how I love being rich. Yes, with a P.O. box, I can have my correspondence forwarded without anyone else knowing. Wire transfers, traveler's checks, it won't be that hard. I love it when a plan comes together.

Alright, little island, whatever your name is. Get ready. Lily Darling will finally have some time to herself to figure out who is trying to end Wendy T. Bell's career. I need a break from this opulent crowd of hypocrites. You all think you've conquered me at fifty? Ha! I'm just getting started!

Being Wendy (In a world afraid to grow up)
Michele Olson© 2021 All rights reserved.
LakeGirlPublishing.com

ALSO BY MICHÈLE OLSON

Mackinac Island Stories

All these stories are stand-alone books but are richer if read in order.

Being Ethel (In a world that loves Lucy)

1979 is getting on Piper Penn's nerves. Struggling to survive past tragedies, she finds comfort in Old Hollywood movies in her native San Francisco. Seeing no reason to adhere to man-made rules after her first-hand look at the ultimate in hypocrisy, Piper does what she wants, and trouble follows.

An unexpected inheritance on a tiny Midwest island in the Straits of Mackinac provides an escape. The mandated stay at the island's glorious Grand Hotel gives her spirits a much-needed boost, especially when she catches the eye of a handsome groundskeeper. Taking part as an extra during the filming of the island movie, *Somewhere in Time*, adds to her excitement about this turn in her life.

When mysterious accusations and headstrong residents send her into a tailspin, she finds friendship from a quirky, *I Love Lucy* loving nun who challenges her embittered look at life and faith. Can Piper survive the baffling attempts to derail her inheritance before it's too late or has she fallen for a well-planned ruse while falling in love?

Being Dorothy (In a world longing for home)

1980 has rattled Dorothy Cooper's world. Disillusioned, she drops off the grid after more than a decade of dedication to The Service, a highly secretive organization. An expert at hiding, being found in less than a year reinforces Dorothy's fear that she is losing her edge.

Escaping to a remote area from her long-ago past along with a fellow Service insider, they both assume new identities on a tiny Michigan island in the Straits of Mackinac. Taking up residence in the opulent Grand Hotel, Dorothy questions their relationship and wonders if anyone can be trusted after what she's seen. Trying to remain in the shadows, loneliness draws her into a friendship at a new knitting and craft shop, The Creative Lilac. The camaraderie and ambiance the owners and frequent visitors enjoy disrupts her concept of marriage, family, and faith.

Can Dorothy find her long-lost feelings of love before the enemies of The Service find her? Or has her past destined her to an endless life-on-the-run, never allowing her to know the happiness of home?

And this book!
> ***Being Alice (In a world lost in the looking glass)***
> **Set in 1981**

Nonfiction

5 Easy Steps to a Happy Birthday!
> ***A practical, funny guide to a Happy Birthday every single year!***

When was the last time, as an adult, you had a gloriously, fun-filled, satisfying, memorable Happy Birthday? If that's not your norm, it's time for a change! Whether circumstances, apathy, or disappointment have pushed you into a world of ho-hum birthdays, this is your chance to recover the bliss of a well-celebrated birthday—on your terms.

Filled with practical suggestions, get ready for an outrageously gratifying, joyous, and "dream come true" birthday—every year. Everyone should have a Happy Birthday, every single year! Get ready to celebrate!

Would you like a personalized signed sticker for you book?

Simply email me. I'll let you know how to get one when you
send a Self-Addressed Stamped Envelope.
Also, a great gift idea!

Are you going to Mackinac Island? Please take some pictures of
my book on the island at different places! Send me some pics of
you and fun book pics. I'll send you a special prize!
info@lakegirlpublishing.com